APR 22

D0481263

NOWHERE TO CALL HOME

Also by Cynthia DeFelice

The Apprenticeship of Lucas Whitaker

The Ghost of Fossil Glen

CYNTHIA DEFELICE

Nowhere to Call Home

Farrar, Straus and Giroux / New York

The author is deeply indebted to Thomas Minehan for his fascinating and informative book Boy and Girl Tramps of America, *published in 1934 by Farrar and Rinehart Incorporated, and for the characters and scenes it inspired in* Nowhere to Call Home.

The author gratefully acknowledges George Deeming, Curator, Railroad Museum of Pennsylvania, for his expert review of the manuscript.

Copyright © 1999 by Cynthia C. DeFelice
All rights reserved
Distributed in Canada by Douglas & McIntyre Ltd.
Printed in the United States of America
Designed by Golda Laurens
First edition, 1999
12 11 10 9 8 7 6

Library of Congress Cataloging-in-Publication Data
DeFelice, Cynthia C.
      Nowhere to call home / Cynthia DeFelice. — 1st ed.
          p.   cm.
      Summary: When her father kills himself after losing his money in the
stock market crash, twelve-year-old Frances, now a penniless orphan,
decides to hop aboard a freight train and live the life of a hobo.
      ISBN 0-374-35552-5
      1. Depressions—1929—Juvenile fiction. [1. Depressions—1929—
Fiction. 2. Tramps—Fiction. 3. Runaways—Fiction. 4. Orphans—
Fiction.] I. Title.
PZ7.D3597No   1999
[Fic]—dc21   98-36602

For Chip, my guide on life's final journey

Nowhere to Call Home

One

*W*ith a start, Frances Elizabeth Barrow awoke from a sound sleep. She sat straight up in bed, her heart pounding unpleasantly. A noise, a loud one, had awakened her. But what, she wondered groggily, had it been? Some part of her brain recognized the sound, but in her muddled state of half sleep she couldn't quite place it. The longer she tried, the more unsure she became about what it had sounded like, or if she'd even heard it at all.

She rang the bell, and Mrs. Bailey, the housekeeper, soon peered in the door. In answer to Frances's question, she said, "It was nothing, miss. Go back to sleep." But her voice shook, her face was pale, and her smile looked ghastly in the dim light of the hallway.

When Mrs. Bailey's footsteps died away, Frances looked at the clock and saw that it was close to midnight. She got out of bed and peered down the corridor. Lights shone from her father's wing of the house. She wanted to go ask him what the noise was and why Mrs. Bailey had acted so peculiar, but she didn't. Father didn't like to be disturbed at night. He didn't like Frances disturbing him at any time, for that matter.

She shut her eyes and listened hard. At first she heard only the ticking of the grandfather clock on the landing and the occasional creak of the big old house's woodwork, but then she detected muffled voices coming from the direction of her father's rooms.

A knock at the front door made her jump with surprise. She hurried to her bedroom window. A police car and an ambulance were pulled up in front of the house, their lights flashing eerily through the drizzle. Running to the top of the stairs, Frances saw Gordon, the butler, in the foyer.

Frances had never before seen Gordon wearing anything but his proper suit and tie. But there he was in pajamas, dressing gown, and slippers, his hair rumpled from sleep. He opened the door to admit three men, two of them in policemen's uniforms. There was a short discussion before the men, accompanied by Gordon, began climbing the stairs.

"Gordon, what was that loud noise?" Frances asked. "Where's Father?"

"Miss Frances!" exclaimed Gordon. Usually so composed and dignified, the butler looked startled and ill at ease. "You—you should be in bed, miss."

"But what has happened?" Frances asked.

"You wait, miss," Gordon said. "In your room. Mary or Mrs. Bailey—someone—will come and . . ." His words came out disjointed and choppy, then trailed off. He added, with a desperate, pleading note in his voice, "*Please*, miss."

Frances was so taken aback by Gordon's odd behavior that she stepped aside at the top of the stairs to let him pass. The three men nodded to her grimly as they, too, walked by. They headed down the corridor toward her father's rooms, and Frances stood frozen with uncertainty and dread.

She didn't want to disobey Gordon, but she couldn't go back to her bedroom and *wait*. She had to know what was happening *now*. After a moment of indecision, she began running down the hallway toward the lights and the sounds and stopped at the door to Father's sitting room.

There the servants—Mrs. Bailey; Mary, the housemaid; Bridget, the cook; even Junius, the stooped old gardener who had been with the family since Frances's father was a boy—were gathered, along with Gordon. The door to her father's bedroom was ajar; Frances could hear the other three men talking in low, urgent voices.

Before the servants saw her, she had a moment to observe their faces. They looked frightened, she thought. She was beginning to feel frightened herself. Their talk stopped when they saw her.

Frances asked the only question she could think of. "Is Father ill?"

Mary gasped and covered her face with her hands. Bridget turned a deep red, and tears squeezed out of the corners of her eyes. "Oh, the poor, wee lass," she whispered. Mrs. Bailey, the housekeeper, stared fixedly at the wall. The others looked down at their feet.

At last Gordon cleared his throat and said, "No, miss. That is . . ."

For a moment, Frances felt like stamping her foot and shouting. Why were the servants acting as if they'd lost their senses as well as their powers of speech? "Father!" she called. "What has happened?" She rushed toward the bedroom door, but, after just a few steps, she found herself lifted up into Junius's warm embrace.

"No, Miss Frankie," he said. "You don't want to go in there."

Junius was the only person who called Frances Frankie, and he did so only when Father wasn't around. Father didn't approve of nicknames, saying they were for the "lower classes." He said that Frances had been given a perfectly good name when she was born, and he expected people to use it. But Frances loved being called Frankie.

6

She almost smiled—until she looked into Junius's face and saw the anguish in his eyes.

The uneasiness that Frances had begun feeling when she'd first awakened fluttered in her throat. She buried her face in the front of Junius's bathrobe, wishing that she could stay right there, with Junius's arms around her and his hands gently patting her back, and never, ever have to listen to whatever it was he was about to tell her.

"Frankie, Frankie, Frankie," he murmured soothingly. "Something bad has happened, Frankie, and I need you to be as strong and brave as you can be. Can you do that for old Junius?"

Frances shivered. Without looking up, she nodded.

"You come on with me, now," he said softly.

Frances walked with Junius down the hallway to her bedroom. They sat together on the davenport, and Junius gazed into Frances's eyes. His own eyes held kindness, and pain. He seemed to be having trouble deciding how to begin.

At last he said, "Miss Frankie, do you recall, about this time last year, folks were mighty upset about something called the stock market?"

Frances nodded. She had heard her father speak of the stock market, though she had no clear idea what it was, and she remembered everyone talking about how it had "crashed." She remembered, too, how tense and ill-tempered Father had been during those days. But what did that have to do with what was happening now, tonight, in her house?

" 'Black Thursday' they called that day, you remember, Frankie? Then came 'Black Tuesday,' right after. It was in all the newspapers and on the radio. Lots of folks had pieces of paper they thought were worth a lot of money. Then, boom! Those pieces of paper weren't worth anything at all."

Again Frances nodded. The newspapers had been full of stories of grown men who had jumped out of windows on hearing that their fortunes were gone.

"Well," said Junius, "that stock market crash helped to bring about what we got now, what's called a depression. That means it's real hard times for lots of folks."

Frances listened, waiting for Junius to start making sense and tell her what was going on in Father's room. As Junius talked, she was dimly aware of voices in the hallway and footsteps on the stairs.

"Now, your father was some smart kind of businessman, you know that," Junius went on. "He kept his factories going when businesses everywhere were closing their doors. But hard times caught up with him, too. He got some real bad news yesterday, Frankie. His business is bankrupt. He lost his money. It's all gone."

Frances shook her head. She couldn't imagine Father "losing" his money; Father was *never* careless about money. He was always telling Frances how important it was for her to appreciate the value of a dollar. He went to his offices each day to watch over his money. Every night he spent hours poring over papers covered with figures. Frances's father knew *everything* about money and how to make it and how to keep it. Poor Father. He must be very sad, so sad that he had taken to his bed.

"Your father was a proud man, Frankie," Junius went on, "proud of all that money he made. And when he lost it—well, I guess he just couldn't see his way to doing without it. Tonight, well—"

"Father!" Frances blurted, wanting only to stop Junius from saying what he was going to say next. Hearing it spoken out loud would make it true, and then nothing would ever be the same again. "I want to see him."

"No, Miss Frankie, you don't want to do that," answered Junius, shaking his head. "A twelve-year-old child shouldn't see a thing like that, no sir. You remember your daddy like he was."

Then Frances's mind grasped the full meaning of the old gardener's words. She heard again the sound that had awakened her and recognized it for what it had been: a gunshot. Her father was dead. He had taken his own life.

Frances was an orphan, and penniless.

Two

$\mathcal{F}$rances lay in bed, still groggy from sleep, watching the raindrops pelt the windowpane. What a dreadful dream she had had! Gazing at the clock, she saw that its hands read several minutes after eleven. Mary had not come at seven-thirty, as usual, to wake her and draw her bath. Bridget had not brought her breakfast tray. She was late for her lessons with Miss Chenier, the governess. Father would be furious.

Then she remembered. It was no dream: _Father was dead._

But that wasn't possible! How could Father be dead? Father, who walked to his office and back each day to maintain his health. Father, who insisted that Bridget cook only nutritious foods and no sweets. Father, who fairly bristled with strength and vigor. She expected that any moment he would walk through the door and say in his booming voice, "What are you doing, lying about in bed? Haven't you anything better to do?"

Father's orders kept everyone in motion, Frances and the servants. He *couldn't* be dead, not Father, or everything would stop.

With a sick feeling she listened to the quiet house: everything *had* stopped.

Suddenly she felt frightened. She got out of bed quickly, got dressed, and ventured downstairs. There was no one about. Finally, drawn by the sound of voices, she crept to the kitchen, where she found the servants gathered in somber conversation.

Frances stood awkwardly at the door. "Good morning," she said uncertainly.

"Good morning, miss," a chorus of voices answered. Bridget hurried to the stove and began spooning biscuit batter onto a large baking sheet. Mary gave Frances a look filled with sympathy. Junius came right over to her and placed his brown, weathered hand on her shoulder. Gordon and Mrs. Bailey looked uncomfortable, standing about in the kitchen. Frances thought she knew how they felt. They were used to answering to Father; now that he was gone, no one knew quite what to do, least of all Frances.

Gordon cleared his throat and spoke. "I've telephoned your Aunt Bushnell, Miss Frances. I expect she'll let us know her wishes."

"Aunt Bushnell?" Frances repeated. "But why?" Bushnell Barrow Hill was her father's widowed sister who lived far away, in Chicago.

"She's your only living relative, miss."

"But—"

"You sit down now, Miss Frankie," said Junius, "and Bridget will fix you some breakfast." He led Frances over to the big kitchen table, sat right next to her on the bench, and poured her a glass of juice.

"But it's almost lunchtime," Frances said. "Where is Miss Chenier?"

"I phoned and told her not to come today," answered Mrs. Bailey. "It seemed best, all things considered . . ." Her voice drifted off and stopped.

"Will she come tomorrow?" Frances asked.

Her question was met with silence. Bridget busied herself whisking eggs and pouring them into a frying pan, and the others avoided Frances's gaze. Finally Gordon said, "We don't know, miss. Your aunt is making the arrangements. She said she'd have to speak to the bank, and that they would send someone over today to tell us what's been decided."

"Who is deciding?" asked Frances, confused. "And what are they deciding?"

"We'll have to wait and see, Miss Frankie," Junius said soothingly. "Now you eat something."

Frances picked at her food. In spite of the late hour she felt no hunger, just an unsettled churning in the pit of her stomach.

Bridget was washing the dishes when the doorbell rang. Frances jumped up from the table and accompanied Gordon to the door, where he admitted a tall, well-dressed gentleman. The man introduced himself as Cleveland Fletcher, lawyer for the bank.

Mr. Fletcher told Gordon to assemble the other servants in the drawing room. Turning to Frances, he said, "And you must be Frances. I'm sorry for your loss. I've been in contact with your aunt. She's speaking with the people at the funeral parlor and asked me to tell you that, in light of the circumstances, there will be no service. She's arranged for you to take the early train to Chicago tomorrow—"

"Tomorrow!" Frances blurted, stunned. "But—"

Gordon appeared in the foyer to say that the servants were ready. Frances followed the men down the hallway to the drawing room and listened, dazed, as Mr. Fletcher announced that the house and its contents were being sold to cover her father's debts. He informed the servants that they were to leave on Friday, when they would receive their final wages.

Silence filled the room. Mrs. Bailey spoke first. "But where will we go, sir?"

Mr. Fletcher looked startled, then annoyed. "Why, home, I suppose," he said.

"But, sir," said Mrs. Bailey, her voice tight, "this is my home. I have no other. Nor do the rest."

"Have you no families to take you in?" asked Mr. Fletcher.

"No, sir," said Gordon. "Miss Bridget's family is in Ireland. Mrs. Bailey is a widow, alone in the world, as I am. Miss Mary was put into service because her family is too poor to keep her. Mr. Junius Washington has lived in this house longer than Mr. Barrow himself."

"Hmmmph." Mr. Fletcher reflected for a moment. "Well, there's nothing to be done about it. You can't stay here. At least you'll have a roof over your heads for a few more days until you get settled somewhere."

"But *where,* sir?" Bridget's question was a wail. It hung in the air for a long moment.

Finally Gordon said, "No one is hiring servants in this depression, sir. People everywhere are out of work."

"Men who once was millionaires are sellin' apples in the street," added Junius.

Mr. Fletcher sighed and said quietly, "I know that. I'm sorry. I have my orders from the bank." He turned to Frances. "I understand your care will fall to your aunt now. You're lucky to have a relative to take you in, do you realize that?"

Frances nodded dumbly. But she didn't feel lucky, not the least bit.

Mr. Fletcher continued speaking. "You'll need to pack up the things you want to take to your aunt's house. Just your clothing and personal items, mind you: everything else will be sold. Do you understand?"

"Yes," Frances whispered, although the only thing she understood was that her life was changing too fast. She had never lived anywhere but in this house with her father, and now she had to leave it for her aunt's. It felt all wrong. She scarcely knew Aunt Bushnell, who had come to Philadelphia just once for a visit. All Frances could recall was her aunt's direct blue eyes and penetrating gaze. Once she had overheard a conversation between her father and her aunt, in which Aunt Bushnell told Father that she was concerned about Frances growing up without a mother.

Frances didn't understand what the fuss was about. Her mother had died when Frances was very young, and Frances didn't remember her at all. She wondered about her mother sometimes, but how could she miss what she had never known?

For as long as Frances could remember, her life had been with Father and the servants and her governess. It had always seemed normal to Frances, safe, solid, and predictable.

Until now.

Three

$\mathcal{M}$r. Fletcher handed Frances a train ticket, saying that the train would leave at 8:40 the following morning and arrive in Chicago at 7:20 the morning after that. Her aunt had reserved a compartment for her, he explained, which meant she had a private room with a window, and her own sink and toilet.

Furthermore, Mr. Fletcher went on, a cab would arrive at eight o'clock in the morning to take her to Broad Street Station. He gave her two five-dollar bills, which, he said, was more than enough for food on the train and for her cab fare, and a piece of paper with her aunt's address and telephone number, which he told her to carry with her "just in case." He advised her to take no more than a few days' clothing, saying that the rest would be shipped to her aunt's house. He reminded her again that she was to take clothing and personal items only, and that the bank owned everything else.

When he left, Frances went to her room to pack. But she found herself wandering from the closet to the dresser and back again, without touching a thing. She didn't know what to take to Chicago; she didn't *care* what she took to Chicago; she didn't want to take *anything* to Chicago because she did not want to *go* to Chicago.

Feeling angry and helpless, Frances pulled a few items of clothing from her closet. Mr. Fletcher could go ahead and sell the rest of her clothes. But she wanted her books. Carefully she chose four of her favorites: *The Adventures of Huckleberry Finn*, the *Uncle Remus* stories, *The Call of the Wild*, and *Great Expectations*.

What, she wondered, counted as "personal items"? How humiliating to imagine Mr. Fletcher accusing her of stealing her own things!

On top of her dresser was a matched set: a hand mirror, a tortoiseshell comb, and a brush, all with silver handles engraved with her initials: "FEB." She had never thought about the value of her possessions before. She supposed the set was worth a lot of money, and wondered if Mr. Fletcher meant for her to leave it behind so he could sell it. Also engraved with her initials was a small sewing box that contained a silver thimble, needles, and a tiny pair of scissors. Defiantly, she placed the mirror, comb, brush, and sewing kit in the pile on her bed.

Mrs. Bailey came to the bedroom door then. The housekeeper's face looked funny, blotched and puffy, and her eyes were red. But Frances was too full of her own misery to pay much attention.

"I thought you could use this to pack your things in, Miss Frances," Mrs. Bailey said, handing Frances a soft carpetbag with a leather handle and brass buckles. "We'll be having luncheon now," she added quietly. "Will you join us in the kitchen?"

"Oh, yes, Mrs. Bailey. Thank you," said Frances, quickly stuffing her clothing, books, and other possessions into the bag.

It had long been her habit, when Father was away, to eat in the kitchen with the servants. Not knowing whether or not Father would approve, and suspecting that he wouldn't, no one had ever mentioned this arrangement to him.

Frances always enjoyed those meals in the big, warm kitchen. Along with the food, there was laughter and friendly teasing and, best of all, music. While Mary did the washing up, Junius played the harmonica and Bridget sang the ballads and folk songs of her native Ireland. Sometimes, in the evenings after the dishes were done, they went into the parlor and gathered around the piano to listen to Frances play.

18

She had been taking piano lessons for six years, and Mrs. Moyer, her teacher, said she had talent and a natural ear. Frances loved playing the piano and, oh, how she loved to listen to Junius play the harmonica!

Once she said she wished she could play like that, and he had insisted, "Why, there's nothing to it, Miss Frankie. With all the piano playing you do, you could pick up the mouth organ in no time."

When Frances had asked Father for a harmonica of her own, he had told her it was a "common instrument, not suitable for a young lady." But one evening Junius had surprised her, holding out his hand and saying, "Go on. Open it."

She'd pried open his fingers and found a harmonica! And he had been right: she quickly learned to play it. Before long, she and Junius were playing duets—always, of course, on evenings when Father was away.

Frances entered the kitchen with Mrs. Bailey, and it was clear there would be no music made that day. The meal was a quiet, solemn affair. Bridget talked about trying to save "a wee bit of money" so she could return to Ireland. Mary said she dreaded seeing the look on her mother's face when she came back home. "Mum's got seven little ones still. She needs my wages, not my mouth to feed."

Gordon and Mrs. Bailey discussed the chances of finding a post where they could work together.

After a long silence, Junius spoke softly. "Me, I'm going

to ride the rails," he said. "Jump me a train and go where it takes me. Gotta be better someplace else. Can't be worse than here."

Mrs. Bailey looked shocked. "Junius Washington, you are not going to become a *bum!*"

Junius smiled wryly. "Not a bum, Mrs. Bailey. A 'bo."

Mrs. Bailey looked at him questioningly.

"A hobo," Junius explained.

"A hobo, a tramp, a bum, what's the difference?" Mrs. Bailey said with a sniff of disdain. "And, what's more, you're far too old to be hopping into boxcars and riding around the countryside begging for food."

"Now, that is precisely the difference between a hobo and a bum," Junius said with a quiet smile. "A bum gives an honest 'bo a bad name. A bum begs and steals and drinks wine and whiskey till he can't see straight. He's shiftless, you see. But a 'bo, he's a man of honor. Sure, he'll hop a freight, but—"

Until then Frances had only listened, but now she looked up eagerly and asked, "What do you mean, 'hop a freight'?"

"Why, Frankie, a tramp's got to get from place to place. He's looking for work, and he's got no home. So he might jump on board a freight train without paying. He doesn't hurt anybody, just takes himself a free ride. And when he comes to a town and knocks at your door, it's not to beg something from you but to see what he can do to earn his supper."

20

"You've worked here almost your whole life, Junius. How is it you know so much about tramps?" asked Mary.

"Oh, they come through now and again, and I talk to 'em," said Junius. "I listen and try to imagine what it would be like, going wherever you please, sleeping out under the stars, free as the wind blowing past your face. Now that I got no work and no home, I been thinking hoboing's something I ought to try."

Frances, too, tried to picture what it would be like to go wherever and do whatever she pleased. She imagined sleeping out under the stars, free as the wind. She wouldn't have to go to Aunt Bushnell's or anywhere else she didn't want to go. "I'd like to try hoboing, too!" she said eagerly.

"Miss Frances, the very idea!" exclaimed Mrs. Bailey.

Junius let out his deep, warm laugh. "Oh, Miss Frankie, that's no kind of life for a young lady such as you, no sir."

"But why not, Junius?" Frances cried. When Junius didn't answer right away, she said, "Is it because you don't think I can work?" She felt wounded. Did Junius think she was—what was the word?—shiftless? "I can work as hard as anybody. I know I can!"

Junius chuckled. "Miss Frankie, I have no doubt you can do whatever you set your mind to."

"Don't be encouraging her, Junius," said Gordon. "It's a foolish enough thing for *you* to be thinking of. Tramping is out of the question for Miss Frances."

"But *why* is it out of the question?" insisted Frances.

"The world is a dangerous place for young ladies," said Mrs. Bailey in an ominous tone. "And that's all we need to say about *that,*" she added firmly.

Frances recognized the look on Mrs. Bailey's face. It said that the matter was settled and there would be no further discussion. Frances had seen even Father submit to the will behind that look. But why, she thought with frustration, were so many interesting things deemed unsuitable for young ladies? And what was so dangerous about a girl riding the rails that Mrs. Bailey wouldn't even *talk* about it?

Four

$\mathcal{F}$rances spent the afternoon in her room, trying to find notes on the harmonica to match the way she felt. Instead of playing a familiar tune, she allowed the music to flow from her heart, producing a melancholy sound that captured her mood perfectly.

Her father's death was beginning to seem horribly real. He had died before Frances had a chance—a chance to *what*? she asked herself. And the answer came: She had always thought that someday, when she was older, or smarter, or prettier, or more graceful, or more accomplished at her lessons, Father would look at her and see, at last, the daughter he wanted. Frances, he would say, come sit by me so we can talk. And he would laugh at the amusing things she had to say, and remark upon her extraordinary wit and charm. He would *see* her. Her, Frances.

Now that day could never come. *Father!* The harmonica fell from her mouth and she cried silently into her pillow.

After a time, her sobs subsided, and ugly thoughts began to creep into her mind. Father had left her all alone, without a home, without a penny. Without his supervision, without his guidance. How could he do that? He had always been so strict. To Frances, it had always seemed as though it mattered deeply to him what she did and didn't do. He had told her there were *rules,* and that it was important for her own good that she follow them.

There were rules for proper conduct, proper speech, proper diet, proper manners. There were rules for a proper education, which was why Frances had her lessons from Miss Chenier instead of attending school. There were rules, Father had always said, for *being a Barrow.*

Frances had never thought to question him or his rules. But now he was gone. He hadn't said goodbye. He hadn't cared enough even to leave instructions about how Frances was supposed to go on by herself. Without his money, he didn't want to live. Frances wasn't enough; she never had been. Deep in her heart, she had always known this.

Words repeated themselves over and over in her mind: *It's not fair, it's not fair, it's not fair, it's not fair.*

It was frightening, the way her sorrow began to transform itself into a horrible, black anger that crawled through her belly like a snake.

A reckless, angry voice said, "Father was a coward." She was surprised to realize that the voice, which had spoken aloud, was hers. "It's true," the voice insisted. Father, who had never seemed intimidated by anything or anyone, had killed himself because he was afraid to live without his money. And suicide was against every rule Frances could think of.

"I guess I'll have to make up my own rules," said the daring new voice that came from inside her. "*I'll* decide what it means to be a Barrow."

That evening, after supper, she stole down to the servants' quarters in the basement and knocked at the door to Junius's room. When he opened it, she said, "Junius, are you really going to be a hobo?"

Junius looked startled, then laughed. "I expect so," he said. "Isn't anybody hiring gardeners, what with the hard times and all." He looked at her with curiosity. "Why you askin'?"

Frances didn't answer the question, but instead asked another. "Can people really do that, hop on trains and ride wherever they want? Work to earn their supper?"

Junius reached out and held Frances by the chin so she was looking right into his eyes. "Now, let me tell you something, Miss Frankie. I surely hope I didn't plant any foolish notions in your head about hoboin'. You got someone willing to take you in, feed you, give you a roof over your head. That's good. You'll be able to continue your studies and your music lessons. You're lucky you got a place to go, a chance to get an education, be somebody."

Frances scowled at him, tired of hearing how lucky she was when it didn't feel the least bit true.

"No, Miss Frankie," said Junius, shaking his head sorrowfully. "Trampin's not for you. It's for folks who got no choice."

"But what choice do *I* have?" Frances protested. "Nobody asked me if I want to go to Chicago to live with Aunt Bushnell. I don't even know her!"

"Your aunt's a fine lady, Miss Frankie. I'd go to her house with you if I could, and that's the God's honest truth," said Junius.

"What about what you were saying before, about being free as a bird, with the wind in your face?" Frances challenged.

Junius's face grew even more somber. "Why, all that was just a manner of speaking, Miss Frankie. Do I look like a bird? No sir, and neither do you. Being free to go anywhere usually means you got nothin' to lose and nowhere to call home. And that's no way to be."

"Chicago isn't home," Frances answered sulkily.

"You don't give up, do you, Miss Frankie?" Junius said, smiling gently and shaking his head. "Listen, I'll tell you what. Chicago is right smack-dab in the middle of the country. There's trains going through there all the time. All the 'boes tell me they been to Chicago." He smiled again. "They call it the Big Chi."

Frances listened, interested in hearing anything the hoboes had told Junius.

"Someday when you're practicing the piano at your aunt's house, old Junius'll come to the door asking can he earn his supper by rakin' the leaves or weedin' the garden. How would that be?"

Frances sighed. Junius was being kind. He was trying his best to cheer her up. Nothing that was happening was his fault. "But can't you take me with you?" she begged. "Please, Junius?"

"If I did that, Miss Frankie, the police would be after me for kidnappin'. And if Mrs. Bailey ever got hold of me— ooweee!" Junius put his hands over his eyes in mock horror, then peered between his fingers at Frances. She couldn't help smiling.

Junius's expression turned serious then. "Miss Frankie," he said, "you give Chicago a chance, you hear?"

Frances looked at his face, filled with kindness and concern, and tried to smile. "Yes, Junius," she managed to whisper.

Back in her own room, she climbed into bed. Lying on her back, she stared at the high plaster ceiling, trying to remember something, anything, about her aunt. In the absence of a clear memory, she saw instead her father's chilly blue eyes and stern expression.

Would living with her aunt be like living with her father? Probably. Her father and Aunt Bushnell were brother and sister, after all. There would be the same rules, the same routines, the same insistence that it was all for her own good. But Frances didn't know what that meant any longer.

Now that her father was gone, Frances could see that it was the servants who had been her real family, even more so than Father, more so, by far, than Aunt Bushnell. And now they—Junius, Bridget, Mary, Mrs. Bailey, and Gordon—were lost to her, too, along with Father.

Junius had said tramping was for people with nothing to lose and nowhere to call home. And that, thought Frances, meant her.

Five

_T_he cab arrived promptly at eight o'clock. From the window of her bedroom, Frances watched it pull up to the house. She knew she should go downstairs, but she didn't move. There was a gentle knock at the bedroom door, and Mrs. Bailey's voice said, "Miss Frances? Your taxi is here."

Still Frances didn't move. "Miss Frances?"

Frances took a deep breath, picked up her carpetbag, and opened the door. "Thank you, Mrs. Bailey," she said. "I'm ready now."

Junius and the other servants were gathered in the foyer to say goodbye. Frances felt herself being swept from one farewell embrace to another. Bridget handed her a bundle

29

tied in a cloth. "It's food for your journey, miss," Bridget whispered as she hugged Frances to her. Mrs. Bailey's crisp, starched shirtwaist crackled against Frances's cheek; the front of Mary's dress was wet with tears. Gordon, usually so dignified, patted Frances's shoulder awkwardly. With a quaver in his voice, he said, "You take good care, Miss Frances."

Junius lifted her right up and held her to him for a long time before setting her down gently on the floor.

Frances had her harmonica in her pocket, and she squeezed it as hard as she could to keep from crying. She looked at the servants one last time. "I won't ever forget you," she said in a choked voice. Then she turned away, picked up her traveling bag, opened the door, and descended the steps to the street.

A chilly November wind blew dry leaves through the streets as the taxi carried Frances to the train station. Her mind was spinning in desperate circles. If only she had more time to think! But the station was just three blocks away. Everything was happening too fast.

Her cab pulled up behind the other taxis, near the busy entrance to Broad Street Station. When the driver announced the fare, Frances paid him forty cents from the money Cleveland Fletcher had given her. He opened the door, helped her to the sidewalk, and set her bag down beside her.

Frances waited to see what he would do next. Had Cleveland Fletcher arranged for the cabbie to come into the station with her and see that she got on the right train? Evidently not. However, he did whistle for a red-capped porter, who stepped right up, took Frances's bag, and asked for her ticket. He examined it and smiled. "You traveling in style, missy. Come with me now, and I'll get you settled."

Frances followed the porter into the huge, bustling building. They climbed a wide, sweeping staircase, passing the Dining Room, the Barber Shop, the General Waiting Room, and the Women's Waiting Room on their way to the track area.

There the redcap turned Frances over to a Pullman porter, who escorted her to her car and led her inside. After placing her bag on the luggage rack, he showed her the workings of the toilet and sink, the fold-down berth, and the window curtains. Then he gave her back her ticket and said, "Conductor'll be around after a while to collect your ticket. Have a pleasant trip, miss."

Frances suddenly remembered seeing Father tipping waiters and porters, and she fumbled in her pocket for her money. She had no idea what a proper tip was. She handed the porter a dollar, and his face broke into a wide grin of pleasure and amazement. "Thank *you*, miss," he said. "You have a *real* pleasant trip now, you hear?"

Frances had never had much reason to think about money. She'd never actually had any money of her own. If she needed something, Mrs. Bailey or her father took care of getting it for her. From the porter's reaction, she deduced that a dollar was a lot of money, at least for a tip.

She looked out the window, then down at the envelope in her hand that held her ticket. "Railroad Fare $29.46, Compartment Fare $23.25, Total $52.71," it said. She opened the envelope and examined the ticket and timetable inside. "Redemption of Tickets," she read. "Tickets unused, or partly used, will be redeemed under tariff regulations at full value."

She held in her hand a ticket that was worth fifty-two dollars and seventy-one cents. When she added to it the cash remaining in her bag, she realized that she had sixty-one dollars and thirty-one cents. If she traded in her ticket, she'd have a lot of money.

The train whistle was sounding. Glumly, Frances stared out the window as the engine hissed and the train pulled away from the station, moved several blocks, and crossed the Schuylkill River. To her surprise, after traveling just a few minutes more, the train came to a stop. The conductor called, "Thirtieth Street Station."

From her window, Frances saw more passengers hurrying to board the train. They looked eager and full of purpose, as if they were headed somewhere important, somewhere they wanted to go.

Before she had time to think any more about it, Frances was on her feet. She grabbed her carpetbag, ran down the steps at the end of her Pullman car, and stepped out onto the platform. Head down, her bag banging against her shins and her heart banging against her ribs, she hurried toward the station, half expecting someone to come chasing after her. No one paid her the slightest attention.

In line at the ticket window, she waited impatiently, looking over first one shoulder, then the other. *Stop it,* she told herself. *No one here knows you. No one cares what you do.* Stepping up at last, she said, "I'd like to . . ." What was the word? She pulled out her ticket and read it quickly. "I'd like to *redeem* this for full value, please."

The man at the window examined her ticket and looked at her. "You just got on the train, miss, at Broad Street . . ." He left his words hanging, a question.

"I know, but I—I've changed my mind. I forgot something," she said.

The man's eyes scanned the faces in the line behind her. "Are you traveling alone?" he asked.

"Yes. I'm going to Chicago to visit my aunt. But I forgot something, and so I'd better go back for it and—and catch a later train."

"Is your aunt expecting you?"

"Yes."

"You be sure and let her know you're changing trains, or she'll worry."

"Yes, sir," Frances said with relief.

But the man wasn't finished. "How about if I just give you a ticket for the train to Chicago later this afternoon, how's that?"

"No, I— If you'll please redeem the ticket, I'll take a cab home from here and get the—the thing I forgot. Then I'll see what my aunt and my—my father—want me to do." Frances wasn't accustomed to lying, and was sure the man could tell that was what she was doing.

But he merely shrugged and said, "All right, miss. As you please. I won't even charge you for crossing the river." He handed her some bills and change and then, to her dismay, signaled for a porter. "Find this young lady a cab, please," he told the redcap.

Frances followed the porter to the cab entrance, where he whistled for a taxi and helped her inside. She felt ready to burst with frustration.

"Where to?" asked the cabbie in a bored voice.

"Just a minute," Frances said, watching the redcap head back into the station. As soon as he was out of sight, she opened the door, jumped out of the taxi, and began to run, the cabbie's startled "What the . . . ?" ringing in her ears.

Six

Frances ran for four blocks before she dared to stop and catch her breath. From the street corner where she stood, gasping, she looked out into the West Philadelphia freight yard. Behind a wooden fence, a bewildering maze of tracks crossed and recrossed, stretching off in the distance as far as she could see.

This was where the freight trains loaded and unloaded and were directed on to their next destination. Unlike the passenger cars, which had windows, plush seats, and electric lamps, these were sturdy, working cars. Some, Frances noticed, were flatcars, piled high with lumber, long steel beams, even automobiles and farm machinery. Others, with sides and tops, had to be the boxcars Junius had spoken of.

She wriggled through a gap in the fence, ignoring the large NO TRESPASSING sign, walked out into the yard, and wandered between the sets of tracks. With interest, she noticed that the huge wooden doors on the sides of the boxcars slid to the side to open and close, and that some of the cars stood empty, with their doors ajar. She liked reading the names painted on the sides of the cars: Southern Pacific, Pittsburgh and West Virginia, Great Northern, B&O, and Union Pacific.

As she walked by a signal tower, one of the trains let out a whistle and a cloud of steam, and began to move slowly down the track. Frances watched the seemingly endless line of freight cars with fascination, sure that it was headed somewhere exciting.

Then, from the corner of her eye, she saw two men emerge cautiously from behind a row of dilapidated shacks that bordered the yard. They looked around quickly and began to run across the yard toward another train, which sat idly by, waiting its turn. To Frances's amazement, they hoisted themselves up onto one of the boxcars, slid the door open, and slipped inside, closing the door behind them.

Hoboes! She was sure of it! They were jumping on board the freight train, just the way Junius had described.

"Hey, you there! What do ya think yer doin'?"

Frances turned to see a husky, red-faced man gesturing

angrily toward her. She stood still, unsure how to answer, as he approached. She could see that he had a wooden bat hanging from his waist.

"Why, you're a—excuse me, miss," he said, looking perplexed. "You're not supposed to be out here in the yard. Are you lost or somethin'?"

"No," answered Frances. "I was looking at the trains."

"Well, this is no place for looking," he said with a scowl. "It's dangerous here, with all the trains coming and going and switching tracks. And you want to watch out for the bums. That's what I thought you was, for a minute—a bum, tryin' to nab a free ride. It's my job, ya see, to keep the bums off the trains."

"But they don't do any harm, do they?" asked Frances.

The guard looked surprised. "They're bums," he said, as if that explained everything. "If a person wants to ride a train, he needs to go into that station there and buy hisself a ticket. That's the policy of the Pennsy, miss, and every other railroad I ever heard of. And, like I say, it's my job to make sure nobody's trespassing in this yard. And that goes for you, too. You'd better come with me."

"That's all right," said Frances quickly. "Thank you, but I'll just go buy my ticket now."

"You do that, miss," said the guard. "A bit of a girl like you has got no business in a railroad yard."

Frances began to walk away quickly. She couldn't help feeling glad that the two hoboes had outwitted the guard, and she felt a glimmer of satisfaction at the thought that by distracting him, maybe she had helped the two men sneak into the boxcar unseen.

As she walked across the yard, excitement grew inside her. She pictured herself sneaking into a boxcar. It had looked easy when the two men did it.

A small part of her brain sounded a refrain of all the warnings she'd been given about riding the rails: *A bit of a girl like you has got no business in a railroad yard. The world is a dangerous place for young ladies. Tramping is out of the question for Miss Frances.*

But no one had told her *why.* Junius had talked about tramping as a grand adventure—until Frances said she'd like to try it. One look from Mrs. Bailey and he'd stumbled all over himself, trying to act as if he hadn't really meant it. But Frances remembered the dreamy look on his face when he'd spoken of hopping a freight. The thrill of those words—*hop a freight*—still filled her.

She stood on the street for a long moment, torn by indecision. And then the answer came, so simple she didn't know why she hadn't thought of it before: if tramping was out of the question for young ladies, she wouldn't *be* a young lady.

She lifted her chin and began walking. After several blocks, she came to what she was looking for. A large sign on a corner building read: GOLDMAN'S CLOTHING FOR MEN AND BOYS. She pulled open the door and went inside.

Immediately a salesclerk approached her. "What can I do for you today, young lady?"

Frances almost ran out of the shop, despite the man's welcoming smile. Instead, she took a deep breath and thought fast. "Please, I need to buy some clothing for my brother. He's just my size. We're twins, you see," she blurted. A part of her marveled at the ease with which lies kept coming out of her mouth.

"Well, well," said the clerk. "Twins, you say? And what did you have in mind? A suit, perhaps?"

"No," said Frances. "Some sturdy clothes, for—for working outdoors."

"Ah, yes, winter weather will be upon us before we know it. I imagine you're looking for something to keep out the cold," the man said cheerfully as he began flipping through several piles of pants. At last he pulled out a dark brown pair and unfolded them for Frances to see. "These woolen trousers are very warm and quite serviceable." He held them up in the air in front of Frances, at the level of her waist. "They look to be about the right size. You can make adjustments with these suspenders, if you need to."

Frances nodded. "I'll take them," she said. "And a shirt."

The clerk helped her to choose a shirt woven in tiny brown-and-white checks, a short, dark green woolen coat, a cap, socks, a pair of undershorts and an undershirt, and a pair of stout, practical shoes. From her money, Frances carefully counted out seven dollars and fifty cents for the clothing, thanked the clerk, and headed back to the freight yard.

Her heart thumped as she carefully scanned the tracks for signs of the watchman. Seeing no one, she ran to a dilapidated shack by the edge of the tracks. Inside, she removed the harmonica from her coat pocket and placed it in her traveling bag. Then she took off the coat, her blouse, pinafore, stockings, and underwear and began stuffing them into the bag. There wasn't room for the coat, so she decided to leave it behind, along with her lace-trimmed underwear. She picked up the new undershorts and undershirt and put them on, followed by the checked shirt. It buttoned on the wrong side, which she found quite peculiar, but not nearly as peculiar as the feeling of putting on trousers.

Frances had never worn pants before. She knew some ladies wore them for playing sports and relaxing around the house, but Father had not approved of the practice. Frances found she liked the way the trousers felt once she figured out how to fasten them in front. They were a little too big around the waist, but the suspenders held them up just fine, and the length was perfect. She put the money in her trouser pocket, then tried on the new shoes. To her surprise, they felt more comfortable than her own.

Finally she placed the cap on her head—and gasped. Her hair!

She reached into her bag and took out the silver hand mirror she had brought with her from home. Holding it away from her body as far as she could, she surveyed her image. She saw either a boy with long, curly dark hair pulled up on the sides and tied with a navy blue bow, or a girl dressed up in boy's clothing. Either way, she looked ridiculous, and was sure to attract attention.

She removed the ribbon and tried stuffing her hair up inside the cap, but she had to muffle a laugh when she saw the way her hair made the cap bulge in a silly lump on top of her head. Quickly she dug through the contents of her bag. She had brought no hats; even if she had, they wouldn't be of a style that a boy would wear. Her comb and brush wouldn't help; styling her hair differently wouldn't do, she realized. She needed to *cut* it.

She rummaged through the bag until her fingers touched the sewing kit engraved with her initials that held the tiny silver sewing scissors. Holding the mirror with her left hand and the scissors with her right, she froze, staring at her image in the glass.

It would be easy to put her own clothing back on, buy another train ticket, and leave for Chicago. If I do *this,* she thought, there's no going back.

Her mouth tightened in a determined line, and she lifted the scissors. *Snip.* She cut a tiny bit from the bottom of the long, dark mass of curls that hung past her shoulders. *Snip.* Another lock, bigger this time, fell to the ground. *Snip, snip. Snip, snip, snip.*

It was a slow, tedious business. The blades of the scissors were only two inches long, and Frances's hair was thick as well as long. She needed three hands, that was the problem: one to hold the mirror, one to lift the hair away from her head, and one to work the scissors. In frustration, she placed the mirror down on top of her bag and continued cutting by feel, lifting a long strand of hair with one hand, cutting it close to her scalp with the other, and throwing it onto the floor of the shack. Slowly she worked her way around her head. *Snip. Snip, snip.*

At last, feeling nothing longer than two or three inches, she figured she was finished. With both eagerness and dread, she picked up the mirror to look.

Her eyes grew wide and her mouth fell open when she saw the image looking back at her. It was her own face that she saw, of course, but it was astounding how different it appeared without the familiar feminine halo of curls. She licked her lips, swallowed, and with one hand swept the hair back off her forehead and to the side, then paused to study the effect. Reaching for her new cap, she pulled it snugly over her head and adjusted it so it came down low over her eyebrows. She narrowed her eyes at her image in the mirror and smiled with satisfaction. Not bad.

She no longer looked like Frances Elizabeth Barrow, that was for sure. The funny thing was, she didn't exactly feel like her, either. In her loose trousers, with her short hair, she felt like a new person, someone rash and daring and free.

Frances found a spot between two abandoned boxcars that allowed her to survey the goings-on in the yard without being seen. A train arrived with a squeal of brakes and clanging of couplings. A while later, another slowly departed, leaving behind trails of steam and pungent black smoke that filled Frances's eyes and nose and throat. Signal markers changed, beckoning trains into the yard, or warning them to stop or to slow down. From time to time, brakemen, switch tenders, water boys, firemen with their scoop shovels for loading coal, dispatchers, engineers, and others passed by, and all the while Frances kept carefully out of sight. She was especially watchful for the guard, who idly swung his bat as he patrolled.

She noticed that every once in a while he disappeared into one of the little shanties, where he remained for several minutes. Frances had already chosen the train and the very car she planned to board. But it seemed that every time the guard went into the shanty, there was someone else around. She knew only that she did not want to make a mistake and get caught; she didn't care how long she had to wait.

When she grew hungry, she opened the bundle of food Bridget had packed for her and ate a couple of biscuits and some cheese. She watched the sunlight move across the yard and begin to fade.

After exchanging a few words with a man who came to take his place, the guard she had spoken with left. The new guard didn't seem to take his duties quite as seriously as the first: he went into the shanty and brought out a chair, where he sat. Unfortunately, he could look straight down the row between the cars where Frances was hiding and the tracks. If she ran for the open boxcar she had chosen to ride, she'd almost certainly catch his eye.

Deciding to wait until night came to hide her movements, Frances sat on the ground, out of sight, and leaned her head against her bag. She must have dozed, because she woke to darkness and a flurry of activity around "her" train. She peeked out and saw clouds of steam coming from the engine. The guard was walking along the entire length of the train, holding a lantern. He appeared to be checking the connections between cars, the wheels, and the track itself, and—oh, no!—making sure that the boxcar doors were shut.

Soon he'd be close to the car that Frances had chosen, a sturdy wooden-sided boxcar whose door hung open just enough for a slim body to slip through. She had to act fast. When the guard stepped between two cars to check the coupling, she ran from her hiding place. She got to the car, threw her bag in, then pulled herself up and into the car. There was no time to close the door behind her, and the guard probably would have been able to hear the sound of it sliding shut, anyway. She scrambled to a dark corner and huddled there, heart pounding, listening to the man's footsteps and to his tuneless whistle as he moved up the side of the train.

When he approached her car, she imagined him shining a light inside and seeing her and dragging her out, saying,

"Well, well, well. What have we here?" She held her breath as he stopped whistling and muttered something to himself. Then he heaved the door shut with a grunt and moved on to the next car.

Frances exhaled with relief. But she didn't move or make a sound until she felt the train lurch forward and heard the rhythmic clickety-clack of the wheels as the train pulled slowly away from the yard, heading west, with its cargo of lumber, steel, coal—and Frances Elizabeth Barrow.

_____ *Seven*

$\mathcal{F}$rances hadn't known it would be so *dark* inside the boxcar. She sat for a while, feeling the car rock back and forth, listening to the steady clickety-clack of the train wheels and trying to stop the rapid beating of her heart. To calm herself, she took out her harmonica and began to play. When she paused for a moment, a voice said, "Nice tune."

The harmonica fell from Frances's hands and clattered across the rusty metal floor of the boxcar. She froze, swallowing a cry, and peered into the thick, stuffy darkness. The voice had risen so faintly over the steady noise of the train's wheels that she almost wondered if she had imagined it.

The car had been empty when she sneaked into it back in the yard, she thought wildly. Hadn't it?

Frances sat still, peering into the darkness and waiting for the voice to speak again. When the train passed through a city or a crossing, bands of light came slanting suddenly between the slats on the side of the car. The whistle blew a warning, indicating a crossing of some kind, and in the faint illumination that filtered into the car, Frances was able to make out the vague outline of a figure seated in the corner opposite hers.

From the pieces of straw scattered on the boxcar floor, and the faint smell of old manure, she figured that the car had been used for shipping livestock. But this was no cow, it was a person. A male person, she was pretty sure, and not very old.

He hadn't sounded menacing or even unfriendly, but it set her nerves on edge all the same, the way that voice had come out of nowhere. And why was he just sitting there, so still and quiet?

Frances stared and stared at the shadowy shape in the corner, but it offered no other clues. Whoever he was, he didn't seem inclined to talk anymore. The eerie silence stretched on and on.

Finally, unable to stand it any longer, Frances cleared her throat and, making her voice as deep as possible, said, "Who's there? I thought this car was empty, except for me." She waited, holding her breath.

"I figured as much," the voice replied after a moment. There was a pause, then he added in the same slow, almost lazy voice, "If you'd known I was here, you'd likely not have told me so much."

What was he talking about? She hadn't told him a thing. She'd merely been fooling around with the harmonica, playing a tune, making it up as she went along. "What do you mean?" she asked suspiciously. "I never said a word."

"Didn't have to," he said. "That was pretty near the saddest, most lonesome-soundin' song I ever heard."

Frances shifted uncomfortably on the hard floor. The conversation was making her feel peculiar.

"This boxcar is about as black as midnight," he went on thoughtfully, "but you was fillin' it up with blue."

A sudden rush of tears flooded Frances's eyes, and she was grateful for the darkness that hid them.

"Been on the rods long?" the voice asked.

"Beg your pardon?" asked Frances.

"How long you been on the drag?"

Frances didn't answer. She didn't want to appear stupid, but this person certainly asked some strange questions.

"Mmm hmm," the voice said, as if in agreement with himself. "Thought so. A punk."

"A punk?" Frances repeated.

"A kid."

"I guess," said Frances. "I'm twelve." Immediately, she wished she'd lied and said she was older. Being a boy made her feel safe; being an older boy would have felt even safer.

"Same age I was when I ran off three years ago," said the voice.

So he was fifteen, Frances thought.

"Green as grass, I was, just like you. But, say, ya snuck past that bull just like a profesh."

Whoever this person was, he'd already figured out she was "green as grass," so Frances decided she had nothing to lose by asking, "What bull? And what do you mean, 'profesh'?"

"Bull, a railroad cop. A profesh is a pro, a professional hobo. Like me," he added, and laughed.

Frances was thinking about being on the road for three years. It seemed like an awfully long time.

The voice went on. "Started out thinkin' I'd ride west, find me one of them thousands of jobs I heard was out there. Figured I'd be a millionaire by the time I was fifteen," he went on, with another laugh.

"What happened?" Frances asked.

He didn't answer. A few minutes passed. Frances had the feeling the boy was thinking back over those years, trying to remember, trying to figure out what *had* happened.

"Ya got a name?" he asked suddenly.

Frances hadn't expected the question, not at that moment, anyway, and she wasn't prepared. But she did know she couldn't give her real name. When she didn't get off the train in Chicago, Aunt Bushnell would report her missing, wouldn't she? And people, maybe even the police, would be looking for her. Frances's mind raced, trying to think of a boy's name.

"Frankie," she blurted at last.

Stupid! she thought. Stupid to say her own name, even if it was only a nickname her family never used. She wished she could take it back, but it was too late. "What's yours?" she asked.

"Stewpot," he said. Frances could hear the grin in his voice. "On account of, in the jungle, ya can always find me right near the food."

The jungle? Frances wondered if the boy was poking fun at her, or was maybe just plain crazy. Food seemed like a fairly safe topic of conversation, however, so she said, "I've got some food with me, if you're hungry."

"Hey, now, there's some good news," said Stewpot. "I feel like a regular Johnny Hollow Legs."

Frances shook her head in the darkness, bewildered by this boy's strange way of talking. But she was glad to have the company, and happy to share her food.

She heard Stewpot get up and walk across the car, then felt a rush of cool wind as he slid open the door. "It's not so cold," he said, "and with the light from the moon comin' in, we'll be able to see our grub." He sat down facing Frances, and she was able to get her first look at him.

As she untied the cloth Bridget had filled for her and took out the remaining food, Frances thought that he wasn't bad-looking, even though his freckled face was streaked with dirt and soot. His hair was lighter than hers and, like hers, was mostly hidden under a cap. He was wearing a shirt under a pair of overalls and a wool jacket, and on his feet were worn black boots.

She didn't have to worry about him looking too closely at *her*. His eyes never left the food as she took out first the remaining biscuits, then the cheese, some pie, and an apple. He whistled in appreciation when it was spread out on the cloth. "That's quite a handout. What'd ya do, hit up an easy mark?" he asked.

Frances nodded; it seemed the safest answer. "Help yourself," she offered. He glanced quickly at her, as if to make sure she meant it, then reached for a biscuit. The whole thing disappeared in his mouth, and he'd swallowed it before Frances had taken a second bite of hers. Not wanting to talk while she was chewing, she gestured for Stewpot to keep on eating.

Instead, he reached into the pocket of his overalls and brought out a knife.

Frances gasped and pushed herself up onto her knees. "Take it all!" she cried.

Stewpot's face held a look of utter bewilderment. Then he laughed. "For cripes' sake, sit down. I ain't gonna bump ya or snipe yer grub." He held up the knife and slowly, deliberately began to slice the cheese, smiling with sly amusement at Frances as he did. Then he carefully cut the apple

51

and the piece of pie in half. "There," he said. "That suit ya?"

Frances nodded, feeling so foolish she wished she could disappear through the floor of the boxcar. Stewpot, however, appeared far too entranced by the sight of the food to concern himself with her embarrassment. He hoisted his half of the piece of pie and shoved it into his mouth all at once.

Frances had never seen anyone eat so fast, and could almost hear what Mrs. Bailey would have to say about such manners. Frances had been hungry before, but never like *that*.

"Have the other," she urged, pointing to the remaining half.

Stewpot, still chewing, looked at her quickly, as if to say, "You sure?" Then, not needing to be asked twice, he swallowed, took the other piece of pie, and ate it.

Frances had some cheese and her half of the apple. When the food was gone, she asked, "Do all hoboes have names like yours?"

"Ya mean a moniker, like 'Stewpot'?" he answered, sounding surprised. "Most do. I guess a few might use their true names. Can't think of any right at the moment, though." After a pause, he asked, "Ya haven't got any makin's, have ya?"

"Makin's?" Frances repeated.

"Cigs, smokes, tobacco, anything like that?"

"No."

"Ah, well, too bad for us. After a feed like that, a smoke hits the spot."

Frances, who had never smoked anything in her life, didn't answer. There was something else she'd been wondering about. "When you're"—she hesitated, trying to remember the words Stewpot had used—"on the drag, can you just make up any name you like?" she asked.

Stewpot nodded. "Or somebody else gives ya one. I got my name the first night out. There was a fellow, Murph, he kind of watched out for me, seein' as I was just a punk like you. It was him who called me Stewpot."

Frances wished she had been named by a real hobo. She liked the idea of Murph watching out for Stewpot and allowed herself the small hope that Stewpot might do the same for her.

"If you were to give me a name, what would it be?" Frances asked. The question was out before she even thought about it, and she felt silly as soon as she'd said it. Why would this boy bother to think of a name for her, a punk kid he'd only just met?

But Stewpot chuckled softly, almost to himself. And, almost to himself, he said, "The way ya was playing that harmonica, if I had it to do, I'd call ya 'Blue.' "

Blue. Frances repeated it to herself. It was odd, for a name, but no more odd than Stewpot. She liked it. "Could you?" she asked quickly. "Call me that, I mean."

"You already got yerself a name."

"But I like 'Blue' better!"

Stewpot laughed again. "All right, then," he said. "Frankie Blue."

"Frankie Blue?" Frances repeated.

"That's right. Put 'em together, like. What d'ya think?"

Frances said it again, enjoying the sound of it. "Frankie Blue." It was a long way from Frances Elizabeth Barrow. "I like it."

"All right, then, Frankie Blue," said Stewpot, "play me some more on that mouth box, would ya?"

Frances found the harmonica on the floor, raised it to her lips, and began to play "Amazing Grace." It was a song Junius used to play, which always made her feel sad and happy and full of hopefulness, all at the same time.

While she played, Stewpot slid the door shut and settled back down in the darkness. When she had finished, his voice came once again from the corner, sounding pleased and drowsy. "That's a mighty sweet song, Frankie Blue, mighty sweet."

Frances smiled at the sound of her new name, and began another tune. She played in time with the cadence of the train as it made its way through the night; she played until she could hear the sound of Stewpot's peaceful snoring, until the hypnotic swaying of the boxcar rocked her into a deep and dreamless sleep.

Eight

$\mathcal{F}$rankie was awake the moment the motion of the train stopped. Daylight filtered into the car through the openings between the wooden boards, and she saw that Stewpot was awake, also, and standing by the door of the car, which he had opened a crack.

"Good morning," Frankie said uncertainly. She began to rise slowly, feeling stiff and sore and cold. At the same time, she felt proud: she had survived her first night as a hobo.

"Mornin' yerself," Stewpot returned. "You was poundin' yer ear like a baby just now."

Frankie thought for a moment, then smiled. "You mean I was sleeping like a baby, I bet," she said.

"Righto. I'm just lookin' out to see if the bulls are glim-min'."

From this Frankie figured he was checking to see if any railroad guards were patrolling the area. "Why?" she asked.

"Are you bughouse? I don't fancy gettin' copped."

"What I meant was," Frankie said with something close to panic, "are you getting off the train now?"

"Sure am," said Stewpot. "This here's Pittsburgh. There's a jungle near here where we can get some grub and maybe a boil-up, too."

Frankie's heart leaped with relief to hear Stewpot use the word "we." She had been afraid that he was going to hop off the train and disappear, leaving her alone. The careless confidence she had felt when she'd first jumped the train had faded quickly.

In the short time she had spent in Stewpot's company, she had begun to realize there was a lot more to tramping than simply sneaking into a boxcar unseen. For one thing, it appeared that hoboes had their own private language, one she needed to learn. She still couldn't imagine how or why they were going to the jungle, but she guessed she'd find out. And if that was where Stewpot was going, it was where she wanted to go, too.

He slid open the door about a foot, stuck his head out and looked around, then slid the door open wider. Sunlight filled the car, and Stewpot stared at Frankie. "Guess you don't need no washin', though, leastways not yet." He laughed and pointed down at his overalls and jacket, which were streaked with soot and dirt. "Wait till ya been on the bum for a while. Them duds'll look like these here."

Frankie laughed, silently congratulating herself on figuring out that a boil-up meant to wash your clothing. She still wasn't sure if Stewpot was talking funny just to tease her, but she meant to show him that she was game. "I sure could use some grub," she said, grinning at him happily.

"You learn fast, kid," said Stewpot, grinning back. "Let's go." He jumped down from the car and ran across the yard toward a grove of trees. Frankie grabbed her bag and followed.

When they reached the safety of the trees, Stewpot turned his back to Frankie and fiddled with the front of his overalls. Soon Frankie heard the splashing sound of Stewpot relieving himself against the trunk of the tree. She quickly looked away, feeling her face turn red with shock and embarrassment.

Where she came from, no one even *talked* about such indelicate matters, never mind performing them in front of someone of the opposite sex. Of course, she reminded herself, Stewpot thought she was a boy. Maybe this was how boys behaved when no girls were around. How was she to know?

She wasn't in her fancy house on Spruce Street, with its modern bathrooms and closed, locked doors, that was for sure.

The worst thing, though, was that Frankie now realized that she also needed to pee, desperately. The sigh of relief Stewpot let out as he buttoned himself back up only made matters worse. But she couldn't pee against a tree like Stewpot! And if he discovered that she was a girl, he might ditch her right then and there, and tell her that tramping wasn't for girls, the way everyone else had.

At the far end of the grove were some bushes with the brown and gold leaves of autumn still clinging to their branches. Without saying anything to Stewpot, she headed toward them.

"Hey!" yelled Stewpot, behind her. "Ya want some?" He reached into the pocket of his overalls and pulled out some tattered sheets of newspaper.

Realizing what he must be thinking, Frankie's face grew flushed all over again. But Stewpot merely handed her the newspaper matter-of-factly and sat down, his back against a tree, to wait for her.

Frankie fled to the shelter of the bushes. Mingled with her relief was a huge worry: if she was going to stay with Stewpot, which she very much wanted to do, how long was she going to be able to fool him?

When she rejoined Stewpot, he pointed ahead. "Up there a ways is the river, and a little ways past that is the jungle. But I just remembered a spot where we can have us a swim."

Stewpot led Frankie to an abandoned stone quarry

58

where one of the pits was filled with water, forming a deep, clear pool. She noticed that as they walked, Stewpot leaned down from time to time to pick up sticks. Most he examined and threw back to the ground; a few he ran his hands over, almost lovingly, before placing them in the bundle he carried on his shoulder. Frankie wondered what made him keep one and toss another away, and why he wanted dirty, broken sticks in the first place, but she had so many questions that she couldn't possibly ask them all.

"Here, now," said Stewpot, proudly gesturing toward the pool, as if he had magically created it with the sweep of his arm. "Ain't that pretty?" Before Frankie could answer, he was taking off his jacket and kicking off his shoes at the same time. Next came his shirt, and then he unhooked the straps of his overalls. Frankie watched as they slid down around his bare feet. She tried not to look at the rest of him, which was bare, as well.

Her face flaming, Frankie directed her gaze to her feet, to the ground, to the trees, everywhere but toward Stewpot. He didn't seem to notice her discomfort. "Last one in's a rotten egg!" he shouted, running toward the edge of the quarry and jumping in. He popped up and called, "Come on! It's not bad once ya get used to it."

The air was warm for November, but still chilly. Nevertheless, a bath would feel awfully good after a night spent in the livestock car, Frankie thought. But she couldn't undress in front of Stewpot! No doubt this was the sort of thing

Mrs. Bailey had warned her about. She couldn't help wincing a little at the idea of Mrs. Bailey—or Father!—seeing her now.

Glancing over toward Stewpot, she saw that he was splashing about, spitting long arcs of water into the air, not even looking her way. She considered for a moment, then began unbuttoning her coat. She had, after all, purchased boy's undershorts and an undershirt. Stewpot might think she was odd for keeping them on, but better he think her overly modest than that he realize she was a girl! Thankful for her straight, slender body beneath the underwear, she jumped in after Stewpot.

He was waiting for her when she surfaced, gasping at the cold. Quickly he reached out and dunked her under. She struggled from his grasp, laughing and half choking, and swam after him to get revenge.

Stewpot was older and stronger, but Frankie was the better swimmer, so they were evenly matched. Frankie was able to swim underwater, as well, which allowed her to sneak up on Stewpot and take him by surprise. After one particularly stealthy ambush that resulted in a good dunking, Stewpot cried, "Uncle! I give!" He swam to shore, pulled himself up on the rocks, and lay facedown.

He was still laughing and panting when Frankie heaved herself up and stretched out on her stomach on the rock beside him, breathing heavily. Stewpot turned his face to

Frankie and sighed contentedly. "That oughtta get the crumbs out."

"Now *I* give," said Frankie. "What're 'crumbs'?"

"Bugs," answered Stewpot. "Lice. You know."

Frankie didn't know, having never had bugs, but she didn't let on. She supposed she'd have them soon—who could help it, sleeping in boxcars and jungles and who knew where else?

Frankie lay shivering until, slowly, the sun on her back and the heat from the rock began to creep through her body. This must have been what Junius had been talking about, this delicious sense of freedom and well-being. The rock felt softer than the floor of the boxcar, and she cracked one eye open to say so to Stewpot. To her surprise, he was dozing, even though they had been awake for just a short time.

When she heard Stewpot stirring, she raised her head and said, "I'm starved."

"That makes two of us," said Stewpot. "Let's hightail it to the jungle and see if they got some mulligan goin'." He sat up and reached for his pants. Frankie turned away to allow him to dress.

The sun had dried the back of Frankie's underclothes. Quickly she pulled on her shirt, trousers, socks, shoes, and coat, and picked up her carpetbag. She had noticed that Stewpot's pack was much easier to manage than hers; he simply rolled up his possessions in his thin blanket and secured it with a leather strap that he threw over his shoulder.

Her bag, on the other hand, was a nuisance. The short leather handle meant she had to hold it down by her side, and she was tired of feeling it bang against her shins. She looked at it in frustration, trying to figure out a more convenient way of carrying it.

"Here," said Stewpot, reaching inside his own bundle and pulling out a piece of rope. He tied it around one end of the bag, then measured out about three feet of rope before looping it around the other end of the bag. "There," he said, handing it back to Frankie. "Now ya can carry it over yer shoulder, across yer back, like. There's times you're gonna need both yer hands free."

As they headed away from the quarry, Frankie adjusted the bag on her shoulder until it fell comfortably across her back. She threw Stewpot a grateful nod. "That's swell," she said.

After they had walked for what seemed a long time, they encountered a group of five, headed in the same direction. It was obvious that the other people, too, were hoboes. Frankie and Stewpot quickened their steps to catch up. As they drew closer, Stewpot called out, "Hey!" and the others turned around to face them.

All five looked about the same age as Stewpot, which surprised Frankie. She had supposed that most tramps would be grown men, men who had lost their jobs. Yet here, counting herself and Stewpot, were seven kids. She had thought her circumstances were unusual, but something must have happened to send so many others away from home, too.

These thoughts flashed quickly through Frankie's mind. But what really shocked her, causing her jaw to drop open with astonishment, was something else. Two of the five young hoboes standing before her were quite obviously *girls*.

_____ *Nine*

*F*rankie stared at the girls, studying them from head to toe with avid interest. One was tall and skinny, with tangled black hair tied back with a cloth. She wore baggy overalls and a shirt, and boots that were worn down at the heels. Her face was streaked with dirt and coal dust. The other girl was a curly-haired blonde, who stepped right up to Stewpot and gave him a flirtatious smile. She was wearing pants, tennis shoes, and what appeared to be several layers of dirty sweaters.

Frankie hung back as greetings were exchanged. It turned out that Stewpot knew two of the boys, Tex and Blink. Tex's drawl made it clear where his name had come from. Frankie tried hard not to stare at Blink. He wore an eye patch that had slid up onto his forehead, and he was struggling to pull it down to cover the place where his right eye was missing. Before the patch was in position, Frankie saw that Blink's empty eye socket looked sore and red. Tears ran from it, and he kept brushing them away with the back of his hand. She wondered how he had gotten such a horrible injury.

"This here's Frankie Blue," announced Stewpot. "He's green, but he's okay."

"Is he traveling with you?" asked the blond girl.

"Guess so," said Stewpot with a smile. "Lucky stiff, ain't he?"

Good-natured jeers answered this remark. Then, pointing to the dark-haired girl, the other boy, and the blonde in turn, Tex said, "These here are Vera, Happy Joe, and Dot."

Frankie listened as Stewpot, Blink, and Tex compared notes about where they'd been during the time since they'd last met up.

"I went down to Lousy Anna," said Blink, "and I can tell ya, I ain't never goin' back. It's no place for 'boes down there. Bulls are mean as snakes and you can't get a handout no matter how good your spiel."

"I've heard that," said Stewpot, nodding his head sympathetically. "Stick to the North, I say."

"Yeah, and freeze your keister," said Vera scornfully, with a toss of her dark head.

"When it starts snowin', I aim to go to California," said Blink.

"I ain't never been there," said Dot.

"Well, don't bother," answered Stewpot.

"How come?"

Stewpot shrugged. "No work."

"So what's new?"

There was sarcastic laughter at that, then silence as the group drew closer to a camp that sat on the riverbank. Frankie wrinkled her nose at the smell from a huge sewer pipe that was spewing waste into the river. Once they had passed the pipe, the smell improved, and Frankie took her first look around the "jungle."

Situated in a stand of trees, it was, she saw, a haphazard grouping of scabbed-together shelters. There were lean-tos made from odd boards, barrels, and crates, and covered over with ragged pieces of tin, or wood, or filthy bedsheets tacked by the corners to the uprights. Sacks of burlap filled with straw lay on the ground, along with a few dirty scraps of blanket.

In roughly the center of the jungle were the remains of a fire, still smoking. Over it hung two large tin cans with long wire handles. Vera picked up several flat tins shaped like dishes and sniffed them. "This is a fine way to leave things," she said with disgust. "Here, you, Blink, take these down to the river and scour them out with sand. Tex, get some wood, and Happy Joe, for cripes' sake, take a bath."

Pointing to Frankie and Stewpot, she said, "You gaffers go get some grub. Me and Dot'll cook it. There's a bakery on the stem might give you some day-olds. But mind you don't bring the bulls down on us."

"Come on," Stewpot said to Frankie. He shot her a sly wink as they headed off. "Bossy, ain't she? But how 'bout that Dot, ain't she somethin' to look at?"

Frankie nodded in agreement, trying to appear enthusiastic, but she was still struggling to get over her surprise at the sight of the other girls. Surprising her still further was the tiny twinge of jealousy she had felt when Stewpot talked about Dot. She told herself she was being ridiculous: She was a boy named Frankie Blue, and Stewpot was her traveling companion.

About a mile from the jungle, Stewpot said it was okay to begin looking for food. That, Frankie guessed, was what Vera had meant about being careful not to bring the cops down on the jungle.

On the outskirts of the city, they came upon a man and his wife, digging potatoes in a field.

"Will you give us a few, mister," Stewpot asked with his most winning smile, "if we dig three or four bushels for you?"

The man and his wife stared.

Stewpot sneezed, then sniffled and wiped his nose with his sleeve. Frankie, thinking that perhaps this was a ploy to gain sympathy, added, "We haven't eaten since last night."

The man and his wife looked at each other, and some sort of silent signal passed between them. "Well, I don't see why not," the man said. They handed their tools, short-handled rakes with four long tines, to Frankie and Stewpot.

Frankie watched Stewpot work and did as he did, raking through the ground to uncover the potatoes, knocking off the dirt, and tossing the potatoes gently into the baskets. The woman disappeared inside the house, while the man toted the full baskets to a truck pulled up by the side of the field.

When they had filled four bushel baskets, the woman returned with a pitcher of milk and began unpacking a picnic basket. Frankie's mouth watered at the sight of sandwiches filled with thick slices of ham, buttered bread with two kinds of jelly, and a jar of pickles. She was wondering whether she and Stewpot would be invited to share the food, when the woman called, "Leave off that work, now, and come eat. I thought with the weather so warm and all, we'd picnic right here."

Frankie turned happily to Stewpot, who was wearing a huge smile. The woman spread a cloth on the grass, and the four of them sat down together.

"Live near?" inquired the man.

"Naw," answered Stewpot. "I came from near Baltimore once. Now I'm on the move, lookin' for work."

The man looked at Frankie, and she mumbled, "Same here."

"There's no work around here, I can tell you," said the man, shaking his head. "We got bread lines and soup kitchens in the city now. Guess you've prob'ly seen it for yourselves. Don't know what this country's comin' to."

"It's hard times, all right," said the woman with a tired sigh. "We won't get much for them taters. But at least we got food, what with all these vegetables we grow."

"Maybe when Mr. Herbert Hoover himself is standin' in a bread line, he'll take notice," the man said bitterly.

"Now, you'll ruin your digestion gettin' all worked up about President Hoover," his wife scolded gently.

Frankie wished they'd talk about it some more. The man seemed to be blaming Mr. Hoover for the hard times, but her father had thought the President was a great man. She remembered one night when Mr. Hoover was giving a speech on the radio. Father had listened to every word, nodding in agreement. "Hoover understands business," Father had said approvingly.

But Father's business had gone bankrupt, she reminded herself. Was it really possible that President Hoover would soon be standing in a bread line?

Frankie's thoughts were interrupted when the woman reached into her apron pocket and handed a handkerchief to Stewpot, who continued to sniffle while they ate. "You can keep it," she said, adding awkwardly, "I got plenty."

Stewpot looked embarrassed. "Thanks, ma'am," he mumbled. "Much obliged."

When they had finished eating, Frankie and Stewpot helped load the remaining potatoes in the truck. Then the farmer said, "You fellers are welcome to all the spuds you can carry."

Stewpot produced a burlap sack, grinned, and asked, "Could we maybe have a cabbage along with them taters?"

Soon the sack was full of potatoes, cabbages, and apples. Stewpot found a stout stick and tied the sack to it, and he and Frankie each carried an end.

"Thank you very much," said Frankie.

"Yessir, we sure do thank you folks," Stewpot added.

"You take care of that cold you've got," the woman called.

"I sure will, ma'am," answered Stewpot. Then to Frankie he said, "Guess we'd better hightail it."

As they walked back to the jungle, Frankie said, "I lied back there about being from Baltimore."

"What of it?" said Stewpot, sounding surprised. "Most 'boes tell ghost stories, leastways to people they don't know."

At Frankie's puzzled look, he explained, "Stories that ain't true, about where they been or where they're goin'." He shrugged. "I figure that's how it is with you."

Frankie nodded, grateful that Stewpot understood and glad that he wasn't one to ask a lot of prying questions. Seeing the other girls had made her wonder if she should just confess that she, too, was a girl. But then perhaps Stewpot wouldn't let her stay with him. She decided to stick with her "ghost story" for the time being, until she knew more about hoboes' ways.

_____ *Ten*

_W_hen Frankie and Stewpot arrived back at the jungle, Vera was tending the fire, feeding it just enough from the pile of wood Tex had gathered to keep it going. " 'Bout time you gaffers showed up," she called. "We was about to eat Tex's boots, only there's not enough leather left on them things to mention."

Tex looked down at his boots and grimaced. Frankie looked, too. She thought they had to be the sorriest excuse for a pair of shoes she had ever seen: broken laces held together a few strips of leather that were barely connected to the thin, worn-down soles.

"Gotta get somethin' to cover my dogs before the snow starts flyin'," Tex mumbled.

"When ya do," Dot called from where she was arranging a straw bag under one of the sheds, "grease 'em up good. That makes 'em last."

"Let's have a look at what you stiffs got," said Vera, pointing at the bundle Frankie and Stewpot carried.

Frankie untied the sack from the stick, and Stewpot proudly held it open. Tex, Blink, Vera, Dot, and Happy Joe gathered around. Tex whistled with admiration.

"Dot, you and me'd better get choppin'," said Vera.

"Too bad we don't have a little meat," Dot said wistfully.

"Meat?" said Blink with a snort. "What's that?"

"Meat's always yesterday or tomorrow," Vera said, "never today." She took a knife from her pocket and began cutting up a cabbage. "You," she said, directing the knife tip toward Frankie, "wash them spuds off, would ya?"

As Frankie walked to the riverbank with the potatoes, she saw three more hoboes approaching the jungle. Back at the campfire, the newcomers, all boys, were offering contributions to the meal. One, who introduced himself as Slim Jim, had three fish; another, named Spit, handed over a bag of day-old doughnuts. The last, a big, strapping boy with red hair who was called Omaha Red by the others, reached underneath his coat and produced a chicken. There were cheers and whistles at the sight of it.

"Looks like Red had him some luck," said Happy Joe.

"How'd ya pull that off in broad daylight?" Blink asked.

Vera was eyeing the chicken warily. "The farmer you nabbed that from—is he gonna be bringin' the coppers down on us?"

"Naw," scoffed Omaha Red. "Whaddya take me fer? A punk?"

Red's remark reminded Frankie of her own lowly status as a punk, and she kept her mouth shut. Besides, it was apparent from the talk that Red had stolen the chicken, and that made Frankie feel peculiar. She hated to think that policemen might come and arrest them, but that wasn't all that bothered her. She and Stewpot had worked hard for the food they brought back to the jungle, and the farmer and his wife had "paid" them willingly and generously. Frankie had felt quite proud of that. It was exactly the way Junius had described hoboing. Stealing—that was another matter.

She watched to see how Stewpot reacted to the stolen chicken. He seemed as happy as everyone else about having a little meat in the pot.

Vera made short work of skinning and cutting up the chicken, and soon the pot was bubbling and the smell of the concoction called "mulligan" had drawn them all into a circle around the fire. Everyone was waiting for Vera to declare the stew ready. The three fish had already been skewered on sticks, cooked, and eaten, along with the doughnuts and most of the apples. But the tantalizing aroma of the stew kept them riveted to their places.

While they were waiting, another tramp joined them, an older man named Peg-Leg Al. He and Tex knew each other and were doing a little catching up.

"Ain't seen you since that time in Cincy," said Tex.

"Ya lost some teeth since then, I see," said Al.

"Yeah," Tex answered with a sigh. "Got in a bust-up with a bull on the Santa Fe. He tried to kick me off, and I kicked back. I guess you could say I won the argument, but I lost the dern teeth while I was at it."

Al nodded sympathetically.

"You got rid a yer crutch and got yerself a leg," observed Tex.

"Yep," said Al proudly, holding his wooden leg up for all to admire. "Made it myself."

Frankie looked at the homemade contraption. Two narrow boards were nailed together at the bottom and held open by a crosspiece at the top. A wad of cloth rested on the crosspiece, and on that rested Al's stump. Pieces of canvas and leather held the leg to Al's thigh, and an extra-wide strap ran up over his right shoulder to hold the whole thing in place.

"Watch how I can hustle on this baby," said Al. He stood up and walked quickly into the deepening shadows away from the fire.

"Ain't ya afraid of slippin'?" called Blink.

"Naw," answered Al, returning to the circle and sitting back down. "I got a hunk a Kelly-Springfield tire on the bottom. When I decide to lam, I leave skid marks!"

He guffawed, and everyone, Frankie included, laughed along.

"Soup's on," Vera announced. "Pass your plates and don't be pushy about it. There's a few spoons that was left here, not enough to go around, though."

Smooth and quick as a cat, Stewpot reached out a hand, grabbed two spoons, and handed one to Frankie. She held her tin of stew on her lap and took a first cautious taste. Her eyes widened with pleasure. Who could have imagined that cabbage and potatoes and the odd piece of chicken could taste so incredibly good? She was quite certain that she had never eaten anything as wonderful as this stuff called mulligan.

The stew and the fire combined to create a relaxed, contented mood around the circle. Vera gave one final order: "This place was crummy when we got here, but we ain't leavin' it that way for the next gang. So clean your tins after, all of ya." Then she settled down to her own plate.

While they ate, they talked, and Frankie listened. A favorite topic was the "bulls," both the railroad police and regular uniformed cops, and tips for outwitting them. The conversation returned often to food: how to get it and how to make it taste better.

"What I do," said Blink, "is, I walk back and forth in

76

front of a restaurant or coffee shop, checkin' out the guys sittin' at the counter. Then I go in and sit down next to one, and I give my spiel to the waitress: ya know, can I wash dishes for a plate and a cuppa coffee. Nine times outta ten, one of the guys at the counter'll say, 'Give the kid a plate,' and pay for it hisself."

Tex nodded approvingly, but Dot said, "*I* try that and, nine times outta ten, the guy'll want somethin' for his kindness, if ya know what I mean."

Frankie didn't know, exactly, but Vera grinned slyly. "Eat and run—fast."

They talked about the hard times that had come to the country. Slim Jim told about actually finding work. "I unload coal all day and the guy hands me two tomatoes. I give 'em back, says, 'If that's all yer givin' fer a day's work, you must need it more than I do.' "

Others had similar stories. Then talk changed to the subject of the upcoming winter, which everyone spoke of with dread.

But to Frankie, sitting on her straw sack next to Stewpot, winter and its troubles seemed far away. She looked up at the sky and thought she'd never noticed how black it was, how bright the stars were, or how close they seemed. The chill of the night air against her back made the fire's warmth on her face feel even more comforting. Her belly was full, and her body felt deliciously tired from the hard work of digging potatoes. She smiled drowsily to herself.

Junius should have seen her today—nobody could call her shiftless!

"Hey, Frankie Blue." A voice spoke loudly in her ear. She started out of her half sleep to find Stewpot gazing at her with a grin. "Wake up and play us somethin' on that mouth organ, would ya?"

"Sure," Frankie said. She reached into her traveling bag, took out the harmonica, and looked around at the circle of faces. "I'm not that good," she said apologetically, thinking of the way Junius could play.

"Just play 'er," said Happy Joe. "It beats listenin' to Vera flappin' her mouth."

Vera turned to give Happy Joe a playful swat, while Frankie played a few practice notes to warm up. She began with "Amazing Grace," since Stewpot had seemed to enjoy it so much the night before. After a few bars, she was pleased to hear someone humming along. Then Dot joined in, singing in a voice that was surprisingly sweet and clear.

"Oh, my," Dot said when the music ended. "I do like that song, but tonight it makes me feel too sad. Could ya play somethin', ya know, a little more lively?"

Frankie played "Camptown Races," followed by every "lively" song she could recall. Some of the others joined Dot in singing from time to time, and Slim Jim and Omaha Red kept time by drumming on their dinner tins.

While Slim Jim, Stewpot, Vera, and Omaha Red had a smoke, Frankie played "Swanee River," sweet and slow and

78

quiet. When she looked up, the flames from the fire had died to a few glowing embers. Vera and Blink were stretched out on the ground on the other side of the fire. Peering into the darkness, she saw lumps that she realized were others rolled up in blankets; the rest, she figured, had gone to find shelter in the lean-tos.

"Wanna flop here next to the fire?" asked Stewpot.

Frankie nodded, putting the harmonica in her pocket. She arranged one of the straw-filled sacks on the ground and lay down. The burlap was scratchy against her cheek, and a musty smell arose from inside. She reached into her bag and took out two articles of clothing; in the dim light she couldn't tell what they were, but it didn't matter. She handed one to Stewpot.

"What's this?" he asked.

"Put it under your head, if you like," Frankie told him. "It's softer than the sack."

"Hmm," said Stewpot, "smells better, too. La-di-da!"

Frankie curled up on her side and snuggled down into the straw mattress. The sadness and desperation of the past few days seemed far away, as if they had happened in a different world. She could feel the warmth from Stewpot's body on her right side, the heat from the fire on her left. She couldn't remember feeling happier.

Eleven

The smell of coffee woke Frankie the next morning. Peg-Leg Al had coaxed the fire to life and started a pot boiling. "Cuppa misery?" he asked Frankie.

"Thanks," she said, taking the tin cup he handed her. Carefully, she took a sip. She'd never tasted coffee before, and she thought "misery" was a good name for the oily, bitter stuff in her cup. It was warm, though, and she wrapped her cold hands around the cup and huddled closer to the fire.

"Got some sand, if ya want," said Al.

Frankie was perplexed by the offer, until Al took a paper from his pocket, unfolded it, and held it out to her.

80

"Sugar?" she asked.

Al nodded proudly. "Take a pinch," he urged.

"Thanks," said Frankie. She sprinkled the sugar in her coffee, stirred it in with a stick, and tasted it. "Mmm. Better," she said with a smile.

She looked around for Stewpot and spotted him on the riverbank, splashing his face with water. Vera, still lying nearby, moaned and rolled over, pulling her blanket up over her head. Dot was heading down toward the river to join Stewpot, and the lumps on the ground that were Happy Joe and Blink began to stir. Omaha Red, Slim Jim, and Spit were nowhere in sight.

Frankie reached for her traveling bag, thinking she'd get her toothbrush and clean up a bit along with Dot and Stewpot. But the bag wasn't where she had left it the night before. She stood up and looked all around, tossing aside the sacks she and Stewpot had slept on. The bag wasn't anywhere in sight. She touched her pant leg and was reassured to feel her money and her harmonica still there.

She tiptoed between the sleeping forms on the ground, but saw nothing except their own knapsacks and bundles. Then, moving outward from the fire in an ever-widening circle, she searched the jungle.

"Hey, where ya goin'?" Stewpot called. His hair was wet and slicked back, and his freckled face was pink from the chill of the river water.

"Nowhere," answered Frankie. "I—I lost something. It

must be around here somewhere . . ." Her voice trailed off as she continued to look in the scrubby brush at the edge of the jungle.

Stewpot appeared at her side, along with Dot and Blink. "What is it?" he asked. "We'll help ya look."

"My bag," Frankie answered. "It's got everything in it, everything I own. Remember, last night I got my harmonica out of it? It was right there where we were sitting. Now it's gone."

Stewpot and Blink exchanged a worried look. "Where's Red and his bunch?" Stewpot asked.

Dot shrugged. "They were already gone when I got up."

"Let's look around," Stewpot said grimly.

They fanned out in different directions. After several minutes, Frankie was relieved to hear Dot's triumphant voice: "I got it!"

Frankie knew she hadn't left her bag way out there, and it certainly hadn't walked by itself. She went with the others to join a grinning Dot, who emerged from the bushes holding up Frankie's bag.

"Thanks, Dot," said Frankie gratefully when Dot handed it over. Examining it, Frankie saw that it was open. She set the bag down and looked through the contents. There were her clothes, toothbrush, and books.

But everything of value, the silver-trimmed brush, comb, and mirror, and the sewing kit that held the small silver scissors, was missing.

Tears stung her eyelids, and she fought to keep them back. "Gone," she said.

"What's gone?" Stewpot demanded.

Frankie looked up at the angry faces of Stewpot, Dot, and Blink. It took a moment for her to realize that they weren't angry with *her* but about what had happened. She described the missing items and watched the anger on their faces turn to puzzlement and awe. Then everyone spoke at once.

"What's a guy want with stuff like that?"

"Where'd ya nab such fancy goods? A jewelry store?"

"Makin' a heist in a jewelry store takes a lot of brass!"

"I didn't steal them!" Frankie cried.

"Red and them's prob'ly already sold the stuff by now." This last remark was from a scowling Stewpot.

"Sold my things?" Frankie asked with dismay.

"Did or soon will," answered Stewpot. "I shoulda warned ya to keep a sharp eye out, Frankie. I didn't like the looks of them from the start."

"Shouldn't we tell the police?" Frankie asked. As soon as the words were out, she realized what a stupid question it was.

"Are you crippled under the hat?" Dot asked scornfully. "Ya think the cops are gonna believe ya ever had that stuff in the first place? They'd figure ya stole it. Same as we did," she added slyly.

"I told you, I didn't steal it!" Frankie said hotly, although she knew Dot was right.

"Okay, okay, don't get yerself riled. So where'd it come from? Lemme guess: you're really a rich swell, like in the nickel pictures, right? And ya just like sleepin' on the ground with the likes of us." Dot shrugged. "Takes all kinds." She turned her back and walked away.

Dot's remark was a little too close to the truth. To hide her discomfort, Frankie said, "What's the matter with her?"

"Aw, you know how frills are," said Blink. "Always givin' a guy a hard time."

Frankie took this opening to say, "I didn't expect to see girls"—she corrected herself—"*frills* on the road, anyway. Isn't it dangerous?"

Stewpot seemed to think about that. "I guess they gotta watch out for themselves more'n we do."

"Vera and Dot both figure they're better off on the drag than at home," Blink said. "They sure got some stories."

"Like what?" Frankie asked, unable to help herself.

"Oh, you know," said Blink. "Vera's mother's boyfriend started messin' with her, so she had to get out. And Dot's old man was mean as a snake, from the sounds of it. When she had bruises on her bruises, she couldn't take it no more."

Frankie wanted to ask Blink more about Vera and Dot, but Stewpot spoke then. "Guess yer stuff's gone fer good, Blue. How 'bout we blow outta here?"

"Sure," said Frankie. "But if I ever run into that Omaha Red, he'll be sorry!"

"You said it, Frankie," said Stewpot approvingly. "Ya wanna come with us?" he asked Blink.

"Where ya goin'?"

Stewpot looked at Frankie. "We ain't talked about it. Anyplace special ya wanna go, kid?"

Frankie shrugged, then added hastily, "Anywhere but Chicago."

"Guess we'll head west," said Stewpot. He winked at Frankie. "Show the kid the country." He turned back to Blink. "How 'bout it?"

"Naw," replied Blink. "I guess I'll stick with Happy Joe and Tex for now. Come winter, we'll prob'ly meet up with ya at one of the missions."

A shadow passed over Stewpot's face. "I don't aim to spend another winter in them flophouses. Them places make me sick. And I already got a cold."

As if to prove his point, he sniffed, cleared his throat, and aimed a gob of spittle off into the grass. "Well, Frankie Blue," he said, "we goin' or not?"

*A*s Frankie and Stewpot made their way back to the railroad yard, Frankie asked, "Did Blink ever tell you what happened to his eye?"

"Yeah," answered Stewpot. "He was ridin' a freight one time, can't remember where. Sittin' on top of the car, ya know, 'cause the weather was nice. Anyway, a hot cinder from the engine came flyin' back and hit him square in the eye."

Frankie flinched, imagining it. "What about Al's leg?" she asked.

"I heard he was flippin' a train and fell under the wheels," Stewpot said.

86

"You mean, he tried to jump on while the train was moving?"

"Yep," said Stewpot. "Us 'boes do it all the time."

Frankie was quiet, thinking about Blink and Peg-Leg Al. Stewpot looked at her and seemed to read her mind. "Aw, don't worry, kid," he said with a laugh. "Look at me. I still got all my parts, right? I'm in swell shape."

"I guess," Frankie said. "Except for that cold."

"That ain't nothin'," Stewpot said. "C'mon, let's go to the bakery and see if they got any day-olds they feel like givin' away."

As they walked the streets, Stewpot gave Frankie advice about asking for food. "Almost any bakery will give you day-olds if they got 'em, but the best time to ask is when they're closing up and got stuff left over they didn't sell, see? Now this morning, they might still have the stuff, or they coulda thrown it out."

In response to Stewpot's request for "anything you was gonna throw out anyhow," the baker gave them some rolls, doughnuts, and a loaf of bread. When Stewpot offered to wash the windows in return, the man in the bakery shook his head. "To tell you the truth, I wish I could give you more," he said sadly. "I've got a boy about your age who took off, too. Had a buddy who talked him into it. I hope somebody's feeding him."

He handed the bag to Frankie. "Thank you, sir," she said. "I'm sure your boy is fine, wherever he is."

"I hope you're right, sonny," said the baker. "I hope you're right."

Outside, Frankie opened the bag, and the smell made her aware that she was hungry again. She handed a doughnut to Stewpot and took a huge bite of one herself.

"Soft," said Stewpot with his mouth full. "Don't even have to dunk 'em."

Frankie had finished her first doughnut and was reaching for a second when Stewpot said, "Take it easy there, Blue. We're gonna be on that train awhile. Gotta make the grub last."

Frankie quickly dropped the doughnut back into the bag, feeling ashamed and still hungry.

"What d'ya say we stop at this butcher shop. If we can get a ring of bologna or somethin', we'll be all set."

The butcher, however, did not share the bakery man's sympathetic feelings. "Get outta here, ya lousy bums!" he shouted, waving his large knife, his face flushing with anger over his bloody-fronted white apron. "And tell yer crummy friends—no handouts at Schumacher's!"

Frankie turned quickly to leave. She knew her face was as red as Schumacher's, red with embarrassment and anger.

"He had no right to call us that!" she said. "He didn't even give us a chance to say we'd work for his crummy bologna. I wouldn't eat it if he got on his knees and begged!"

Stewpot was looking at her with amusement and a glimmer of admiration. "Pipe down there, Blue," he said. "Better get used to bein' called a bum."

"Why should I?" asked Frankie indignantly.

"That guy there, there's lots like him."

"Well, they ought to watch what they say," muttered Frankie.

"What they say don't matter none as long as you know what you are and what you ain't. It's when ya start believin' 'em, you're in trouble. Then ya start hoistin' the booze, and before ya know it—you're a bum for real. I seen it happen to a lotta guys."

Frankie was still fuming about the butcher. "How would *he* like being out of work?" Suddenly she thought about Junius, Mary, Bridget, Mrs. Bailey, and Gordon. It was . . . she had to think a moment . . . Oh, no, it was Friday, the day Mr. Fletcher had told the servants they had to be out of the house.

She remembered Mrs. Bailey's puffy face and red-rimmed eyes, and the panic and shock on the servants' faces when Mr. Fletcher made his pronouncement. She heard the echo of Bridget's wail, and of Mrs. Bailey's question, "But where will we go, sir?"

At the time, Frances had been so caught up in her own misery that she hadn't given the plight of the servants much thought. She turned to Stewpot and said, "People don't ask to lose their jobs and get thrown out on the street!"

"Hey, Blue," said Stewpot, "you're right, but it ain't worth gettin' riled about. We got to see if we can find us some more grub before we head for the yard."

Frankie looked at Stewpot's matter-of-fact expression and tried to swallow her anger. The butcher and Cleveland Fletcher had both shown the same indifference to people who couldn't find work. Guiltily, she realized that all she had done was complain about having to go to Chicago. She hadn't said even a word of condolence to the servants. What would become of them?

She thought about the hoboes who had come to her house and visited with Junius. She had never been aware of them. Had Father, she wondered. Probably not. She felt sure Junius had fed them. Would Father have approved? Or would he have said they were bums and turned them away? The questions made her feel uncomfortable. She was afraid she knew the answers.

She and Stewpot stopped at a small corner grocery, where the owner said she'd give them some cheese if they swept the floor and moved some heavy boxes in the stockroom. Back out on the street, they unwrapped the cheese and saw that it was moldy around the edges. But that didn't bother Stewpot. "We'll cut off the green stuff and she'll be fine," he said cheerfully. "Now I got one more stop to make, and then we gotta haul tail to the yard." He added suddenly, "You got a knife?"

"No," answered Frankie.

"Too bad," said Stewpot. "A 'bo needs a knife."

"I have a little bit of money, though," Frankie said eagerly. "How much does a knife cost?"

"You, Frankie Blue, are jest full of surprises. Where'd you get your hands on money? Steal it from home before you left?"

Frankie thought about that. "I guess I did," she said finally.

"Well, how much ya got?"

"About fifty-four dollars," Frankie said.

Stewpot's jaw dropped. He gave Frankie a long gaze, then whistled. "That's mighty big money, Frankie. Ya know, you're lucky Omaha Red didn't make off with it."

"I know," said Frankie.

"Ya better watch yer back, walkin' around with dough like that. Where ya keepin' it?"

"In my pocket."

"Well, put it in yer shoe. And don't tell nobody else ya got it."

"Okay," said Frankie humbly. Stewpot waited while she untied her shoe, folded the bills, and placed them, along with the coins, in the shoe.

"How . . . ?" Stewpot shook his head. "Never mind. Ya got more than enough for a knife, that's fer sure, and I know jest where ya can get one. Come on."

He led Frankie for several blocks to a less-prosperous section of town. They went into a shabby little shop that was full of merchandise of all kinds, jumbled together in piles so high that at first Frankie didn't see the tiny man with a skinny mustache perched behind the counter on a stool.

"Ya got any pocketknives?" Stewpot asked him.

"Sure do," answered the man. He smiled without warmth. "You got any money?"

"Sure do," answered Stewpot with a nod in Frankie's direction. "Leastways, he does."

"What did you have in mind?" the man asked, reaching beneath a display case and pulling out a tray.

"Well, I—" Frankie stopped, having no idea what she had in mind.

"Like this here," said Stewpot, reaching into his pocket and taking out his knife. "One that folds and closes up. See, like this. Not too big, but with a strong blade."

The man set the tray down on the counter so Frankie and Stewpot could look. There were several knives, along with watches, pieces of jewelry, odd-looking coins, medals, and eyeglasses. None of the items, Frankie noticed, was new.

She reached for a knife about the size and shape of Stewpot's, fit her fingernail into the little slot on the blade, and opened it. The blade was shiny and looked sharp. Stewpot reached out and ran his finger along it, nodding with approval. Frankie rubbed the handle. It was beautiful, she thought, smooth and milky white.

"Mother-of-pearl," the man said proudly, as if he'd made the knife himself.

"How much?" Frankie asked.

"Two dollars," the man answered.

Frankie reached down to untie her shoe and get the money, but, to her surprise, Stewpot said scornfully, "Highway robbery, that's what that is. Come on, Blue. Let's go."

Frankie stood, astonished, as Stewpot turned and began to walk away. He was almost out the door and Frankie was about to follow him when the man said, "All right. One dollar."

Stewpot turned around. "Twenty-five cents," he said.

"Seventy-five."

"No deal."

"Fifty."

"Twenty-five or nothin'," replied Stewpot. "And I'm only offerin' that much 'cause of that fancy handle."

The man sighed deeply. "You drive a hard bargain, kid," he said, shaking his head. "All right. You can have it for twenty-five cents. Not a penny less, though," he added.

"Twenty-five it is," said Stewpot happily. "Pay the man, Frankie, and let's get goin'."

Out on the street again, Frankie held her knife in her palm and admired it. "I never saw a store where things were old and used like that. And where you tell the man what you want to pay instead of him telling you!"

"Ain't you never been in a pawnshop?" asked Stewpot. Frankie shook her head.

"Folks who need money go there with things they figure they can do without, and that guy pays 'em for their stuff. Then he tries to sell it to somebody else. Or maybe the person who pawned it in the first place will come back when he's got some dough and buy his own stuff back."

Frankie thought about that. "What if you return to buy your stuff back and somebody else already bought it?"

Stewpot shrugged. "That's your tough luck."

Frankie ran her hands over the smooth mother-of-pearl handle of the knife in her pocket, hoping that whoever had pawned it didn't care much about it and wouldn't come back to find it gone. She didn't say anything to Stewpot, though. He might think that was a sissy thing to think. Instead she said, "I was about to pay him two dollars."

Stewpot stopped walking and poked his finger at Frankie's chest for emphasis. "Ya never give a pawnbroker what he asks for right off. He'll try to get ya to pay five times what somethin's worth. Ya just keep bargaining till he won't go no lower."

"How did you learn that?" Frankie asked.

"It's jest the way it is," Stewpot answered.

Frankie nodded, silently thanking her lucky stars for the good fortune of joining up with Stewpot. She wished she could do something to pay him back for everything he had done for her.

"Hey!" she said. "I know what. You take a dollar and seventy-five cents. If it wasn't for you, I wouldn't have it anymore, anyway. You're the one who bargained for it."

"Naw," said Stewpot. "Keep it."

"Take it," said Frankie. "Please."

"I said keep it," Stewpot said gruffly, and he stuffed his hands in his pockets and began to walk away.

Frankie stood for a moment watching him go, realizing that she had offended him and afraid that he wanted nothing more to do with her. She ran to catch up. "Stewpot," she began. But her voice came out high-pitched and pleading, sounding too much like a girl's. She fell into step beside him and didn't say anything.

Stewpot broke the uneasy silence. "Look, Blue. You're still pretty green. If somethin' happens to me and ya get in a jam, you're gonna need that dough. That's all I'm sayin'."

"But nothing is going to happen to you!" Frankie exclaimed, finding herself terrified at the thought.

"Course not. I'm jest sayin', hang on to yer dough and watch yer back."

Frankie nodded to show she understood. Then, to change the subject, she asked, "So what's this other stop you want to make before we catch the train?"

"Oh, yeah," said Stewpot, his face brightening. "It's right up here. You'll see."

Frankie breathed a silent sigh of relief and followed him to the door of a small shop. The sign read, A. L. WELLS,

TOBACCONIST. In smaller letters were the words CIGARS, CIGARETTES, TOBACCO, PIPES AND ACCESSORIES. Puzzled, Frankie followed Stewpot into the shop. She knew he liked a smoke when he could get one, but she didn't think he had money to buy cigarettes or tobacco.

"Good morning, Mr. Wells," Stewpot called out as they entered the dimly lit store, which was filled with the rich, sweet smell of many kinds of tobacco. "Ya got any empties for me?"

"Well, well, well. It's been a while, young man. And, yes, I've saved a few for you."

Frankie watched as the short, stout shopkeeper disappeared into the back room. He continued speaking, his voice sounding muffled and distant. "Some other—er, travelers—have come in asking, but I told them, 'No, these boxes are promised.' " He reappeared, carrying a stack of five wooden cigar boxes, which he set down on the countertop.

"Hot diggety dog!" Stewpot declared. "That's mighty nice of ya, Mr. Wells. Now, how the heck am I gonna carry 'em all?"

Mr. Wells glanced at Frankie. She introduced herself. "I'm Frankie Blue and I'm pleased to meet you, sir."

The tobacconist returned her smile and said, "Likewise, Mr. Blue."

The name Mr. Blue startled her at first. Then she smiled at the sound of it. Turning to Stewpot, she said, "I can probably fit three in my bag." She leaned down and opened the bag, rearranging her possessions so that she was able to stuff three of the boxes inside. There was more room, she thought ruefully, since the heist. She supposed she could throw out her old clothes. At some point, when Stewpot wasn't watching, she would. After all, what did Frankie Blue need a blouse and pinafore and stockings for?

"There," she said to Stewpot. "Now you can roll up the other two boxes in your bundle."

"No problem," said Stewpot happily as he did exactly that. He hoisted his bundle by the strap and tossed it over his shoulder. "Thanks, Mr. Wells," he said. "Now what have ya got for me to do? Got any deliveries?"

"No, no," said Mr. Wells. "Take the boxes and go, young man. Where are you fellas headed?"

"Frankie Blue here's got a hankerin' to head west," answered Stewpot.

"Well, mind you be careful," said Mr. Wells. "People have been raising a fuss about vagrants lately, and the police are under pressure to crack down and make arrests."

"We'll be careful," Stewpot reassured him. He turned to leave. "Thanks for the boxes, Mr. Wells."

"And the advice," added Frankie.

"Goodbye, fellas," said Mr. Wells. As they walked through the big wooden door, he called after them, "And good luck to you both."

"C'mon," Stewpot said. "We gotta hurry. But don't run.

Just walk real casual-like till we get outta town so we don't attract any attention."

"Okay," said Frankie, trying her best to imitate Stewpot's nonchalant stroll. "I give. What are the boxes for?"

Stewpot smiled mysteriously. "You'll find out," he said, "soon as we get settled in a boxcar, headed west."

Thirteen

*A*s they walked toward the railroad yard, Stewpot said to Frankie, "Most trains that head west go by way of Big Chi."

Frankie remembered Junius telling her that "Big Chi" was the hoboes' name for Chicago.

"But don't worry," Stewpot went on. "Ya said ya don't want to go there, so we won't. It makes things kinda tricky, but I got it all figured. We'll head from here to Cincy, then to St. Louie. Then we gotta decide." He looked at Frankie. "Ya wanna go to San Fran or ya wanna go north?"

Frankie wished she had paid more attention to her geography lessons with Miss Chenier. Stewpot seemed to know the name and location of every city in the country. It made her feel ignorant by comparison. She knew San Francisco was in California, and she remembered Stewpot saying he had been to California. Perhaps he'd rather go somewhere else. "What's north of San Fran?" she asked.

"Well, there's Seattle," said Stewpot. "That's about as far north and west as ya can go. Unless ya wanna go to Canada or someplace," he added with a question in his voice.

"No," said Frankie uncertainly. She didn't feel ready to go to a whole different country. "I—I don't think so."

Stewpot snapped his fingers suddenly. "I got it!" he said. "From Cincy we'll go to St. Louie and from there to St. Paul and then we'll just keep goin' north and west till we get to Montana."

He was starting to get excited; Frankie could hear it in his voice. "Murph told me once he took the Great Northern through the Rocky Mountains in the snow, and he said it was the prettiest sight he'd ever seen on this earth. That's what he said—I can still remember! And Murph saw lotsa places, believe you me. What d'ya say, Frankie Blue?"

Frankie nodded eagerly. She had never seen any big mountains, just pictures of them in books such as *Heidi,* and she wondered if the Rocky Mountains looked like the Alps, where Heidi lived.

Having a purpose, even one so vague as seeing the Rocky Mountains, made her feel better somehow. When she'd first decided to go tramping, she hadn't anticipated how frightening it would feel to be out in the big, wide world with nowhere in particular to go and nothing in particular to do.

Her life up until now had been planned by her father; her days had been scheduled with lessons and meals served at certain times. She had not expected to miss the routines of her old life, and was surprised to find herself recalling them with fondness. A sudden image of herself, sitting happily beside Mrs. Moyer on the piano bench, filled her mind.

She and Stewpot were drawing near the yard, and Frankie was surprised to see about ten other hoboes standing along the tracks.

"Ah, so that's how it is," said Stewpot glumly.

"Why are they all standing around like that?" asked Frankie.

"We're gonna have to flip 'er," said Stewpot.

"You mean we have to jump on board while the train's moving?" asked Frankie uneasily. She remembered Stewpot saying that this was something hoboes did all the time, but she hadn't really thought about having to do it, especially not all of a sudden like this. She was used to getting lessons in doing things, and having time to practice. Hoboes, she was discovering, often got only one chance.

Stewpot nodded, scowling. "It's not hard, Blue. Trouble is, we'll really have to scramble, what with all these other fellers tryin' to get aboard, too."

"But anyone can see us out here, and them, too," she

said, pointing to the ragged collection of hoboes waiting by the track. "Won't someone stop us?"

"It's kind of like a game, see?" answered Stewpot. As he spoke, his eyes were darting left and right, taking in the situation along the track. "The railroad bulls can't let us parade right into the yard and climb on the train. That'd be like sayin' it was swell with them if we all ride free. But sometimes they're willin' to pretend like they don't see us jumpin' on after the train leaves the yard, see? 'Cause the city cops has told 'em they want us all outta town and the sooner the better. This way, everybody's happy, everybody does their job. It makes it a little harder on us 'boes, but what do they care if one or two of us gets flattened?"

Frankie detected a rare hint of anger in Stewpot's voice. "We're not going to get flattened," she said with much more assurance than she felt. "But you'd better tell me what to do."

"Right," said Stewpot, with a flash of his usual good-natured grin. "Now, the thing about this situation here is that the train's headin' uphill as it's pullin' out of the yard. That means she'll be goin' nice and slow. So here's what I wantcha to do. You walk up the tracks, say as far as that buncha trees there." He pointed to a place about one hundred yards farther along the tracks. "When she starts comin', I'll get on first, make sure I got a good hold. Watch how I run alongside the train, then do the same when she gets near to where you're at. I'll holler when I get close, and when I get to ya, I'll reach down to give ya a hand up. Got it?"

"Are we going to ride all the way to Cincinnati hanging on to the outside of the train?" Frankie asked.

"Hope not," said Stewpot. "Ya can usually get the door open. If not, we'll have to hop to another car."

Frankie had a vision of Stewpot and herself "hopping" from one car to another on a moving train, unable to get into any of them. In her imagination, the train picked up speed and they held on for dear life as the day grew colder and became night. She shuddered and pushed the vision away.

An image of Peg-Leg Al, who had lost his leg while trying to jump on a moving train, filled her mind, and she forced herself to push that thought away, as well.

A signal sounded, and the train began to move, very slowly, toward them. "Go!" urged Stewpot.

Frankie ran up the tracks to wait. As the train left the yard, she saw the hoboes who were spread along the rails begin to run. They looked so small! How would they ever reach up high enough? But there! One man jumped and managed to pull himself up—he was aboard! Another jumped up and missed a handhold. He fell to the ground, rolled, quickly got up, and began running again.

For a moment, Frankie lost sight of Stewpot. Someone

had tripped on a railroad tie. Frankie, thinking the fallen figure was Stewpot, felt her heart lurch. But then she spotted him, still running with the others.

She pictured Peg-Leg Al lying helpless as the train wheels crushed his leg, and thought wildly, *I can't do this!* Frozen with panic, she stood motionless. The train drew closer. Stewpot, on board now, was waving frantically, urging her to *run*. She pictured the train, with Stewpot on it, passing her by and disappearing around the bend, leaving her alone. That thought galvanized her. Forcing Peg-Leg Al from her mind, she hitched the strap of her bag securely across her chest and began to run alongside the train.

Already it was gaining speed. She ran, trying not to trip on the uneven rocks or crossties of the railroad bed, trying not to look at the wheels turning so close by, trying only to stay on her feet and to listen for Stewpot's voice over the clatter of metal against metal and the train's shrill whistle and the hissing of the engine.

Then, coming up from behind, she heard Stewpot's voice: "Atta way, Frankie. Okay, now, turn around. See me? See my hand?"

Still running, Frankie looked up to see Stewpot, hanging on to the railing on the boxcar door with one hand, leaning down as far as he could, stretching out his hand toward her. She reached up, but Stewpot's hand was too high, too far away.

"Jump!" he called. "Jump!" His face was distorted in a

104

grimace as he shouted and bent down even farther. Frankie reached her hand up and jumped. She missed Stewpot's hand, regained her footing, jumped again, missed again. Desperately, her breath tearing in her throat, she jumped once more—and felt Stewpot's hand close around her wrist.

When her feet left the ground, she felt as if her arm were being pulled from her shoulder socket. *"Hold on hold on hold on hold on hold on."* She didn't know if Stewpot was calling to her, or if it was her own voice saying the words over and over and over. Gritting her teeth, she held on.

Then, with a ferocious burst of energy, she bent at the waist and flung her legs up so that her heels caught on the narrow platform that ran along the bottom edge of the boxcar, where Stewpot was precariously balanced. She rested for a moment, holding on to Stewpot with both hands. She made the mistake of looking down between her legs, and saw the ground passing rapidly beneath her. Quickly she closed her eyes.

Opening her eyes again, making herself look nowhere but into Stewpot's anxious, encouraging face, she pulled herself up to stand, breathless and shaky, beside him.

Clinging tightly to the metal railing that ran along the middle of the sliding door, she took a couple of deep breaths before turning to look at Stewpot.

"You okay?" he asked.

Frankie nodded. "You?" she managed to say.

"Sure. Now, hang on while I see if we can get in. I shoulda noticed this was a reefer." He turned to face the boxcar and bent down to tug at an iron bar that ran the length of the door at the level of his shins. Holding on with one hand, he reached into his pocket with the other and took out his knife, which he used to do something to the latch on the bar. Finally there was a loud clang. Stewpot gave a whoop of triumph, slid the door to the side, and stepped inside.

Frankie followed. As her eyes adjusted to the semidarkness, she heard Stewpot exclaim, "Hot diggety!" He tossed something toward her. She caught it and realized that it was an orange.

"The whole car's full of 'em!" Stewpot said happily, already tearing the rind from the fruit he held in his hand. Frankie looked around. He was right. Crates of oranges, held in place by netting, were everywhere. Frankie filled her nostrils with their clean, sweet scent and laughed with relief and delight at being alive—alive in a boxcar full of oranges!

The train picked up speed with a sudden jolt, and Frankie fell to the floor, which made her laugh even harder. Stewpot, laughing, too, pelted her with oranges until another jolt sent him to join her on the floor of the boxcar.

When they had recovered enough to speak, Stewpot said, "I wasn't sure ya were gonna make it, Blue. But it wasn't bad fer yer first time, not bad at all."

"Thanks," said Frankie, not knowing what else to say, and not wanting Stewpot to know how horribly afraid she had been. "What were you doing to the door?"

"Aw, they lock up reefers, so I had to break the seal. It's a pain in the tail, but sometimes it's worth it. 'Cause in a reefer there's usually *food*." Grinning, he held up an orange.

"We're in a *reefer*?"

"Yeah. A refrigerator car. Can'tcha feel it?"

Now that Stewpot mentioned it, Frankie *could* feel it: the air in the car was cool and dry. "Won't we freeze?" she asked.

"It ain't a *freezer*," Stewpot said. "I reckon it ain't any chillier in here than it was outside last night. And we got plenty to eat!" He was already peeling another orange. Frankie reached for one, too. Her mouth and throat were parched from running along the dusty track, and the cool, sweet juice tasted wonderful.

She looked at Stewpot to tell him so. He was grinning at her: a piece of orange peel covered his teeth, and he was bugging out his eyes and wiggling his eyebrows. Laughing, she reached for a piece of rind to make her own orange smile. By the time she turned to show Stewpot, he had placed sections of the peel over both eyes, and was groping blindly toward her with his hands extended.

Frankie collapsed helplessly, giggling until she nearly choked. When she caught her breath, Stewpot slapped her on the back and said slyly, "Orange you going to thank me?" which set her off again.

They sat on the floor of the boxcar, watching the scenery from the still-open door, eating oranges until their mouths ached from the sweet-tart juice. Stewpot had decided that since it was about the same temperature outside the car as it was supposed to be inside, no harm would come to the oranges if they left the door open for a few hours. As they swayed contentedly with the rhythm of the train, Frankie suddenly remembered the cigar boxes.

"Hey," she exclaimed. "How about telling me what those boxes are for?"

Stewpot observed her with a look of mock sternness. "I don't know if you're ready yet, Blue," he teased, trying hard to frown. "Only us honest-to-goodness, real, true hoboes know this stuff. You're still awful green."

"I flipped a train today, didn't I?" Frankie challenged.

"I reckon ya did, at that," Stewpot said, still sounding skeptical.

"And I flopped in the jungle and worked for my mulligan, didn't I?" she demanded.

Stewpot could no longer hide his smile. "All right, all right, I'll show ya." He reached into his pocket, took out his knife, slowly drew out the blade, and held it up, testing its sharpness with his thumb. "Now we'll see what you're made of, Frankie Blue. Get out yer knife."

Fourteen

Frankie tried to look casual about drawing her knife. She trusted Stewpot. Of course she did. She remembered how she had flinched the first night she'd met him, when he'd first taken out his knife to cut the food, and how amused he had been to see that she'd thought he might harm her.

But what were they going to do with their knives? Was this some kind of game boys played? And would her ignorance of it make Stewpot suspect that he was traveling with a frill? Part of her wanted to tell him the truth, anyway, so she could stop pretending. But there never seemed to be a good time to come out and say it.

She waited anxiously while Stewpot rummaged in his bundle and came out with something that he handed to her. "Have a gander at that," he said.

Frankie leaned closer to the open door, where the light was brighter, to examine the object in her hand. It was some kind of wooden toy. She looked up at Stewpot inquiringly, but he just looked back, as if to say, "You figure it out."

Frankie looked more closely and drew in her breath in amazement. The toy was made from a single stick of wood. Still long and thin, it had been decorated with intricate, carved designs at each end. But what was in the middle made Frankie shake her head in wonder.

A round wooden ball rattled about in what resembled a cage made from thin bars of wood. The ball was inside the cage—but the bars of the cage were much too close for the ball to fit through. Whoever had made this thing had carved away wood from the stick to form the bars, then continued to carve carefully inside the bars until all that remained was the ball. It was incredible, it was impossible—and there it was, right in her hand.

"That's amazing!" cried Frankie. "Who made—don't tell me *you* made this!"

Stewpot nodded, looking proud and embarrassed at the same time. "That one's called 'Bird in a Cage,'" he said. "Here, have a look at this."

He handed Frankie a wooden chain. Each link was

hooked to the next, and each was perfect and unbroken. The chain, too, had been carved from a single piece of wood.

Frankie smiled. "This is why you were picking up sticks at the quarry," she said. "You use them to carve things like this."

Stewpot nodded. "There's some basswood and cedar trees around there. They're the best for whittlin'."

Frankie gazed admiringly at the two objects, so simple-looking, yet so clever. "How in the world do you do this?"

"Piece of cake once ya get the hang of it," said Stewpot modestly.

"How did *you* learn it?" Frankie asked.

"Murph taught me," Stewpot said. For a moment, his eyes had a faraway look, and his face was sad. "Murph taught me lotsa stuff," he added softly.

"What happened to him?" asked Frankie.

Stewpot didn't answer. "Ya wanna learn whittlin' or not?"

"Yes," Frankie said eagerly, seeing that Stewpot didn't want to talk anymore about Murph.

"Here," said Stewpot, reaching once again into his bundle. He handed her a wooden box.

She opened it and looked inside. "It's empty."

"No kidding," he said with a grin.

Puzzled, Frankie looked more carefully at the box itself. "It's really beautiful." Then, afraid she sounded too girlish, she added, "I mean, it's nice. It's a nice box."

Stewpot looked disappointed. Frankie looked again. "It's a cigar box!"

"Bingo," said Stewpot.

"At least, it *was* a cigar box," said Frankie. "Now it's a—it's a—well, it's like a little treasure chest." She examined the box, trying to figure out what Stewpot had done to make it so beautiful. "You took one cigar box . . . and built up the sides and top with all these thin layers of wood. It looks like they're made from the sides of other cigar boxes."

Stewpot nodded encouragingly.

"Each layer is smaller than the one before, so they make these pyramid shapes," Frankie continued. "And you used your knife to make notches all around the edges of each layer . . . and you put one layer on top of another . . . and tacked all the layers together with little nails. Right?"

"Bingo again!" said Stewpot.

"Do you think I could do it?" Frankie asked.

"Get them boxes and we'll get started," said Stewpot happily.

Frankie reached for her bag. "Have you made other things, too?"

"Sure. Ya can make all sorts of stuff. I do picture frames and little boxes, mostly. I made one kinda big chest, even had drawers in it, with fancy white knobs. They was real porcelain."

"What did you do with the boxes?"

"Sold 'em," Stewpot said with a shrug. "Or traded 'em for grub or a place to flop."

Frankie nodded, beginning to see how whittling might be a good thing to know how to do. "I'd have liked to see that chest with the little drawers," she said.

"I took it door to door when I was done. At the second place, the lady saw it and went bughouse for it. Gave me two bucks," said Stewpot proudly.

Frankie thought about that. Two dollars was a lot of money to a hobo. Two dollars could buy eight pocket knives, or twenty quarts of milk, or forty loaves of bread. She knew that now from listening to Stewpot and from reading the signs in the shops.

It was something she'd never paid attention to before. She'd never had to be concerned about the price of food, or whether or not she could afford to eat. She thought of all the times she had pushed her plate away because she didn't like what Bridget had cooked for her. Her cheeks felt hot as she remembered.

Stewpot, meanwhile, was looking longingly at the boxes of oranges. Frankie wondered how he could possibly be hungry for still more, but he surprised her by saying, "Those fruit crates are what ya need if ya wanna make somethin' big like that chest of drawers. Course, ya gotta be able to stay in one place long enough to finish somethin' like that, and that ain't easy."

"Where did you make the chest?" Frankie asked.

"Chicago," answered Stewpot. "There's a mission there that lets ya stick around if ya work." He sighed tiredly. "But I aim to keep movin', Frankie. I don't care to spend another winter in them flophouses, with their crummy swill and all them stinkin' stew bums pukin' and fightin' and coughin' all night long."

Frankie felt a stab of real fear. The mission did sound awful. But how would they make it through the winter moving from place to place? Hard as she tried, she couldn't picture it.

"I'll never shake this lousy cold in one of them places," Stewpot added glumly.

"Maybe we should get you some medicine," said Frankie.

"Eatin' oranges is s'posed to be good for ya, right?" asked Stewpot. "So I been takin' plenty a medicine! Now, ya wanna try yer hand at whittlin' or not?"

Frankie nodded. Demonstrating as he spoke, Stewpot showed her how to use her knife to dismantle a cigar box. Then he made tiny, even cuts along the edge of one of the sides, removing small pieces of wood shaped like V's.

"Now you try it."

He watched as Frankie made her first few tentative cuts. "That's it. Keep goin', all the way around. We got a coupla more hours of daylight. We'll make a buncha pieces. Later, when we're flopped somewhere for a while, I'll show ya how to put 'er together."

Frankie was quiet as she concentrated on her whittling. For a while it occupied both her mind and her hands, but after she'd gotten the hang of the repetitious notching, she found her thoughts turning to the many questions she wanted to ask Stewpot.

"What's a stew bum?" she ventured.

"An alky stiff. A booze hoister. Ya know, a drunk."

"Oh," said Frankie. She recalled that Father occasionally sipped something called sherry on cold winter evenings, and she remembered a celebration in the kitchen once, when champagne had been served and glasses raised in a toast to the New Year. But she didn't think that was what Stewpot was talking about.

"If ya stay on the drag, you'll see plenty of 'em," Stewpot said. "But that ain't gonna happen to me, Blue. I got plans."

"What are you going to do?" Frankie asked.

"I figure these hard times gotta end sometime, right?" Frankie didn't know about that, but she nodded, wanting Stewpot to keep talking. "And when that happens, I'll get me a job in a factory somewhere, save up some money, and then ya know what I aim to do?"

Frankie shook her head.

"I'm gonna buy me a little farm, raise me acres of spuds and corn and red tomaters. And I'll have cows for milk and meat, and chickens and pigs, and I'll always have a full belly and never have to ask nobody fer nothin'. And when I get married and children come, they'll never have to leave home 'cause their daddy's outta work and there's no money to feed 'em. And I won't never start hoistin' the booze and knockin' my old lady and my kids around like it's their fault there's no jobs and no money and no food."

Stewpot had begun talking faster and faster and with more and more emotion, and he stopped suddenly and swallowed. He gazed out the door of the boxcar, rather than at Frankie.

Frankie realized that Stewpot had told her something about himself, even if he hadn't known he was doing it. But all she said was "It's a good plan, Stewpot."

She thought about Stewpot and his dream, and understood that it was the thing that gave him hope and kept him going, even when the dream seemed impossibly far away. He was planning for the future.

It was late afternoon by then, and getting cold. In the fading light, Stewpot's face was filled with shadows. He was still staring out the doorway, but Frankie knew he wasn't seeing the gaunt, bare trees or the low, gray sky or the light snow that was just beginning to fall. He was looking somewhere else, somewhere Frankie could only imagine.

Suddenly he turned to face her. "How 'bout you, Blue? Ya got a plan?"

Frankie was startled by the question. "Well, I—" She stopped. She had wanted to see what it was like to be a hobo, to sleep out under the stars. She hadn't thought beyond that, had never stopped to consider what it would be like to be on the road for three years, the way Stewpot had, or to think about what might come after.

The truth was that, ever since she had played in her first piano recital at age eight, she had dreamed about being a concert pianist when she grew up. She loved playing in front of other people, being carried away by the music. She enjoyed seeing the shining looks on the faces of the people in the audience, and she liked hearing their applause.

She was seized by a sudden, fierce longing to feel her fingers on the keys. She could almost see herself sitting on the piano bench, with the metronome ticking the beats of the music.

With a pang, she wondered if she would ever have a chance to play the piano again. It wasn't something she had considered when she ran away.

Frankie felt Stewpot's eyes on her. "Hey, Blue," he was saying. "You okay? You were lookin' kinda funny there fer a minute."

Frankie forced a smile. "Yeah, I'm okay. But I guess I don't have a plan, Stew, not really."

"Now, that's a dern shame," said Stewpot. "If I didn't have my farm to think about, I'd probably go bughouse."

Frankie nodded. She knew Stewpot was right. But when she tried to peer into her own future, her imagination failed completely.

Fifteen

_W_anting to put an end to her disheartening thoughts, Frankie stood up abruptly, closed the boxcar door, and sat back down on the floor. She was very hungry. "How about some of that grub?" she suggested.

Stewpot pulled out the food and trimmed the mold from the cheese. They sat munching quietly.

"I sure wish we had a light," Frankie said.

"Don't tell me you're scared of the dark?" Stewpot teased.

Frankie snorted to let him know she was nothing of the sort. "No, I was just thinking that if there was some light, we could read."

"Read what?"

118

"I've got some books in my bag."

Stewpot didn't answer right away. Frankie could feel him hesitating in the darkness. "I got a candle," he said finally.

"You do?" Frankie said excitedly. "Where is it?"

"Hold yer horses and I'll get it."

Frankie could hear Stewpot fumbling in his bundle. Then she heard the scratch of a match, and the soft glow of candlelight illuminated Stewpot's face. He tipped the candle sideways until melted wax ran into a puddle on the boxcar floor, then stuck the candle in the puddle and held it there until the wax hardened. "That do ya?" he asked.

"It's swell," said Frankie, feeling around in her bag and pulling out her books. "Here, you pick which one you want."

"Naw," said Stewpot. "I don't like readin' all that much."

"But have you ever read this one?" Frankie urged, holding up *The Adventures of Huckleberry Finn*.

"Nope."

"I bet you'd like it. And this one—"

"I told ya, didn't I?" Stewpot interrupted. "I don't go fer that readin' stuff."

"But I—" Frankie stopped. She loved to read and was used to spending most of her leisure hours doing so. She found Stewpot's attitude difficult to understand, but if he wasn't interested in reading, she supposed that was his business. "Well, I might read for a while, if you don't mind."

"Why should I mind?" said Stewpot shortly. He was acting awfully touchy all of a sudden, but Frankie couldn't think what she might have said to upset him, and his face was outside the circle of light, so she couldn't make out his expression.

"You feel okay, Stew?" she asked.

"Yeah," he said. "My throat's kinda sore, is all."

Frankie didn't think that was all that was bothering Stewpot, but she didn't know what else to say. She looked down at the books in her lap, trying to decide which one she felt like reading.

"That one looks good," Stewpot said in a low voice, pointing to the colorful picture on the cover of the *Uncle Remus* stories.

Surprised, Frankie handed it to him. "Here."

Pushing it back, Stewpot said, "Naw. You."

"You want *me* to read it?" Frankie asked, confused. "You mean, *out loud*?"

"Yeah," said Stewpot, adding quickly, "unless ya don't want to."

"No," Frankie said eagerly, "I do." She remembered how Mrs. Bailey used to read to her at night when she was little, and how she had loved lying snug in her bed, listening. She opened the book. She had to hold it right down on the boxcar floor, with the candle in front of it, being careful not to burn her fingers, or the pages when she turned them.

Stewpot shifted about, lying on his back and arranging the bundle beneath his head for a pillow, as Frankie read.

She had read all the stories many, many times, but she never grew tired of Brer Rabbit's sassy tricks. Stewpot seemed to enjoy them, too, laughing out loud from time to time, while she read three stories in a row.

Finally she said, "My eyes are about to give out reading in this candlelight. Do you want to take a turn?"

Stewpot yawned. "Naw, I'm gettin' kinda sleepy."

Frankie yawned, also. "Me too." She put the book away and blew out the candle, then settled next to Stewpot in the small area that wasn't taken up by orange crates.

Stewpot was quiet, and Frankie wondered if he was already asleep. She wondered as well what time it was. Time, she reflected, didn't seem to exist once you were inside a moving boxcar. Day and night, morning and afternoon, bedtime and mealtime all lost their former significance. There was only the darkness and the cold and the steady noise of the wheels below, and the feeling of hurtling through space toward an unknown destination.

Without Stewpot, Frankie thought, she'd be frightened and lonely. But, as it was, she could almost feel his strength and courage and assurance becoming part of her.

"Ya know," Stewpot said in a slow, drowsy voice, "that Brer Rabbit, he's littler than Brer Fox and Brer Bear, so he's got to be smarter. I was thinkin'—it's kinda like us 'boes. The cops and the bulls, they're bigger than us, and richer than us, and they got all the other big, rich, powerful guys on their side. And we're like rabbits, tryin' to run and hide and stay outta their way, and still get by. Gotta be tricky when you're a 'bo," he murmured, his voice so full of sleep Frankie could barely hear him. "Gotta be real tricky." His voice faded away, and Frankie could hear him breathing unevenly in his sleep.

She lay for a while in the darkness before drifting off. She awakened once, from a dream in which she was a rabbit running along a railroad track, being chased by foxes and bears with human faces. On and on she ran, looking for her hole, but she couldn't find it. There was nowhere to hide, nowhere that was safe. The creatures were about to catch her in their sharp, gleaming teeth when she woke up, shivering with cold.

Stewpot still slept, breathing through his mouth. From time to time, he coughed a deep, rattling cough. Frankie lay beside him, trying not to listen. She rolled into a ball, hugging herself to try to stop the shaking. It was a long time before she fell back to sleep.

Sixteen

"We're slowing down," Frankie said.

"Yeah," Stewpot agreed. He rose stiffly and stretched in the gloom of the boxcar. "Must be right outside Cincy," he said. "Get ready."

"Ready for what?" Frankie was getting up stiffly, too, after lying all night on the cold floor.

"We gotta jump off before she pulls in. We'd never make it past the bulls in the yard. With all them other 'boes on board, somebody's bound to get copped."

Frankie swallowed. She'd jumped onto a moving train; now she was going to have to jump off one, as well. Stewpot was easing the door open, and Frankie was astonished to see snow covering the ground, the trees, and the roofs of buildings. "It's so beautiful!" she cried, forgetting to lower her voice.

But Stewpot was gazing out the doorway, his eyes darting everywhere, taking in the situation. "Good. We're still outside the yard. We'll wait till we get a little closer, up by them water towers, so we don't have to hoof it so far in the snow. I'll tell ya when to go. Don't forget your stuff," he warned.

Frankie's thrill over the snowfall quickly ebbed. "So I just—jump?" she asked, trying to sound as though the idea didn't bother her at all.

"Yeah," said Stewpot, his eyes still directed up the track. "Keep yer knees loose and, if ya hafta, roll when ya hit the ground. Ya wanna land out away from the train, not close to the tracks, if ya know what I mean."

Frankie, looking down at the tracks and remembering the wheels clanking relentlessly over them, knew what he meant.

"We'll wait till she slows down jest a little more." He paused, gauging the speed of the train. "Jest a little more . . . a little more . . . Okay, let's go." And without another word, he jumped from the train and, remaining on his feet, slid down the bank of the raised railroad bed. He turned quickly and looked up to see Frankie, still clinging to the railing of the boxcar door.

"Hurry, Blue," he hollered. "Jump!"

The train had slowed down to almost a crawl as it approached the signal towers on the outskirts of the Cincinnati yard. But to Frankie the ground seemed to be moving past at an alarming rate. Worse, Stewpot appeared to be growing smaller and smaller as the train moved away. If she remained on board, she'd be caught by the railroad bulls and maybe taken to jail! She *had* to jump.

Do it, she urged herself. *Now. Go.* But nothing happened. Her fingers clung to the railing, not even feeling the cold metal. Her feet didn't budge from their solid position on the boxcar platform.

"Blue!" Stewpot's voice was growing faint, but she could hear the urgency in it.

The train's whistle sounded loudly, startling her into action. Holding tight to her bag, she closed her eyes and jumped. Her right leg crumpled under her and she fell, and her knees struck the sharp cinders beneath the thin blanket of snow. She rolled down the bank and lay still for a moment before opening her eyes. When she did, Stewpot was running toward her, a worried look on his face.

"Blue? You okay?"

Frankie nodded, unable to speak for a moment as she measured the pain in her right leg. She sat up, then got to her feet, keeping her weight on her left leg and slowly shifting some to the right. "My leg is okay," she said. Looking at the tear in the knee of her pant leg, she added, "Better than my pants, anyway."

"I got stuff for sewin' up holes," said Stewpot with a smile. He turned and headed toward a stand of trees. Frankie, knowing by now what he was up to, walked behind an abandoned storage shed that backed up to the tracks. There she squatted with relief, then rubbed her hands and face with snow, washing up as best she could.

Joining Stewpot again, she asked, "What do we do now?"

"You tell me," returned Stewpot.

"Well," said Frankie slowly, "I guess we ought to walk the rest of the way into town, see if we can find some food, and then find out which train is going to—where are we going from here?"

"St. Louie."

"Right. St. Louis."

"Let's go," said Stewpot.

All around them were other hoboes who had jumped from the train. Frankie watched as they slipped off behind trees and buildings and slowly disappeared. She and Stewpot, too, were away from the tracks now, out of plain sight, making their way inconspicuously toward the streets of the city. Frankie plunged her hands into her coat pockets to warm them, but there was no way to keep the wind from coming through the hole in the knee of her trousers.

Stewpot didn't know the city of Cincinnati as well as he'd known Pittsburgh. "This looks like the main stem," he said when they got farther into town. But they found

126

themselves unwelcome at the stores where they stopped to ask if they could earn some food. Finally Stewpot said, "The heck with this. Come on."

They wandered away from the main part of the city, out into less congested areas, where the streets were lined with small but neatly kept homes. As they walked, Frankie noticed Stewpot carefully examining the fences, gateposts, mailboxes, and trees that marked the edges of each yard. She began looking, too, although for what, she didn't know.

"Lookee there," said Stewpot with a grin. He was pointing to the corner post of a picket fence that bordered the property where a white house with black shutters stood among some pine trees.

Frankie looked and saw a crude picture of a cat—just two circles, one for the body and a smaller one for the head, with pointed ears, whiskers, a tail, and four stick legs. It appeared to have been scratched right into the wood. If she hadn't been looking for it, she thought, she'd never have noticed it.

" 'Boes leave marks for each other," Stewpot explained. "Ya just scratch it with your knife, or draw with a hunka coal, or whatever ya got. To warn other 'boes about bad stuff, like cops or mean dogs, or to tell 'em where to go." He smiled and raised his eyebrows, pointing again to the post. "*That* means a nice lady lives here. C'mon. Maybe we'll get lucky and have a real sit-down."

He opened the gate and began walking up the path to

the door. Frankie followed, feeling peculiar about knocking at a stranger's door. She remembered Junius telling about the hoboes who had come to the door. Had there been a mark of some sort outside her house?

Stewpot knocked. After a moment, the curtain on the door was pulled aside, and the face of a young woman peered out. Frankie smiled, trying to look as friendly as possible and wondering, suddenly, if her face was dirty. Stewpot was grinning widely also. The woman's face softened, and the door opened.

"Why, hello, boys," the woman said.

"Hello, ma'am," Stewpot and Frankie said, almost in unison. Frankie spoke up next, wanting to show Stewpot she was learning. "We were wondering if we could do some work for you, ma'am, in return for something to eat."

"You look cold," the woman said. "Why don't you come on in first and warm up?" In the background, a baby began to cry, and the woman pointed them toward the kitchen and excused herself. "You make yourselves comfortable at the table there, and I'll be right back."

"A lotta ladies wouldn't leave the likes of you and me alone for the blink of an eye," Stewpot remarked, wiping off the seat of his pants before sitting down. "Afraid we'd swipe their stuff."

"Shhh." Frankie hushed him nervously, not wanting the woman to hear them even talking about taking advantage of her kindness.

128

The crying stopped, and the woman returned, explaining, "He's fussy sometimes when I first put him down." Then, getting out a skillet, she said, "What about some bacon and eggs and toast first, then you can clear off my front walk. How does that sound?"

"Mighty good, ma'am," answered Stewpot.

Frankie nodded in agreement.

The woman pointed toward the sink. "While I'm fixing it, I'm sure you boys would like to wash up."

"Yes, ma'am," answered Frankie. She glanced quickly at her hands and was ashamed of how filthy they were. The warm, soapy water made her long to soak, as she used to, in the deep tub in her bathroom at home. How long had it been, she wondered, since Stewpot had had a hot bath? How long before she would ever have one again? The question made her feel uneasy; she had no idea of the answer.

Frankie returned to her chair, and Stewpot took his turn at the sink. Her mouth was watering at the smells of bacon sizzling in the pan and eggs browning in butter.

As she cooked, the woman chatted pleasantly about the weather: what a surprise the snow had been and how cold it was for this time of year. "I couldn't help but notice the hole in your trousers," she said to Frankie. "There's a pair of pants upstairs that my husband never wears anymore. You're welcome to them." She said it easily and quietly, trying to be kind without embarrassing Frankie, adding, "He's not a big man. They might not fit too badly."

"Oh, no," Frankie began to protest. Then she felt Stewpot kick her under the table. Startled, she looked up to see him nodding vigorously. "Take 'em," he mouthed silently.

"I hate to think of those pants going to waste when you could use them," the woman said, placing the food on two plates and bringing them over to the table.

"Thank you, ma'am," Frankie said quickly. "For the food—and the pants. That is, if you really don't mind."

"Not at all," the woman said warmly. She poured two tall glasses of milk and set them in front of Frankie and Stewpot. "I'll just run up and get them while you eat."

Frankie dug into the food on her plate. With her mouth full, she said to Stewpot, "You didn't have to kick me!"

Stewpot, too, was eating ravenously. Around a huge mouthful of egg and toast, he said, "One thing ya gotta learn, Blue. If somebody wants to give ya somethin', *take it.* Even if ya don't want it, somebody will. Ya can trade it or sell it or use it to bribe yer way out of a situation, maybe. Ya got it? You're on the bum now."

Frankie nodded. She got it.

The woman returned, the pair of pants over one arm and her baby boy in the other. "He doesn't feel like a nap today," she said, handing the pants to Frankie. Looking down at the baby, she cooed, "He doesn't want his nappy, does he?"

The baby crowed happily and waved his little fists, and Frankie, Stewpot, and the woman all laughed. Frankie rose and carried the dishes over to the sink.

"That grub was top-notch!" Stewpot told the woman. "If you tell me where yer shovel is, I'll start on that walk."

The woman pointed out the window to a shed in the yard, and Stewpot went outside to begin working. To Frankie she said, "Would you like to put those pants on now? It's awfully cold to be walking around like that. There's a bathroom right around the corner there."

"Yes," said Frankie gratefully. In the bathroom, she put the pants on over her others. She rolled up the cuffs, which were too long, and attached her suspenders to the waist. That way, they didn't fit too badly, and the extra layer of warmth would be welcome.

Putting her coat back on, she started to leave the room, then stopped. She looked at the gleaming white toilet bowl and sink, the clean, fluffy towel on the rack, the sweet-smelling soap in the dish, the brightly colored hooked rug on the floor. At that moment, she wanted never to leave that warm, clean, safe room. The idea of going back out into the snow and the cold and the uncertain future seemed horribly bleak.

In the kitchen, she thanked the woman again for the food and the trousers and for welcoming them into her house. To her surprise, the woman's eyes filled with tears. "Don't thank me," she said softly. "I look at you boys and I look at my baby here, and I can't help but think: What if hard times catch up with him someday? I have to hope he'd be treated kindly."

Frankie nodded, feeling her own eyes growing wet. Being here with this woman was making her think of spending time with Bridget and Mary and Mrs. Bailey in the big, warm kitchen at home. A wave of homesickness and regret passed over her. She wondered suddenly what the kitchen and the bathroom at Aunt Bushnell's house looked like, and pictured them warm and clean and cozy. Quickly she pushed the image out of her mind, ran to the door, and let herself out before she began to cry.

Stewpot was shoveling the last of the snow from the front path. "Hey," said Frankie, "I was going to do half the work. Fair's fair." She had intended to shovel the entire walk because Stewpot hadn't been feeling well.

"Too late," he said with a grin. "It was a piece of cake, anyway." But his breath was coming in ragged bursts, and his eyes looked tired.

The front door opened and the woman appeared again, holding a bag in one hand, the baby in the other. "Some food for the road," she called.

Frankie went to get the food and asked, "Is there anything else you'd like us to do?"

"Not a thing," said the woman.

Frankie thanked the woman again while Stewpot put the shovel away. "Guess we're set to go," he said. "Let's see if we can find us a train to St. Louie."

Seventeen

$\mathcal{F}$rankie and Stewpot walked to the railroad yard. This time they approached by the west end, to catch a train going in their direction. They encountered a small group of hoboes headed the opposite way and stopped to talk.

There were five men of various ages. Frankie couldn't tell how old they were, really, but they were a lot older than Stewpot, she decided. With them was one girl. It was hard to tell her age, too, because of the dirt that streaked her face and the hat that was pulled down low over her forehead. Frankie guessed she was fifteen or sixteen. The girl's hair was long and tangled, and looked as if it hadn't been washed in a very long time. One side of her face was horribly scarred.

But what struck Frankie, causing her to stare without realizing it, was the lifeless expression on the girl's face. Her eyes were hollow and dull, her mouth a thin, flat line. She took no part in the discussion, and didn't even seem to hear any of it, as Stewpot, Frankie, and the men talked about their travels, the time of the next train, and the likelihood that the bulls would be watching it closely. The girl stood, staring blankly, seeming to see nothing at all.

"That freight's got a waybill posted for St. Louie," offered one of the men. He pointed to a train on the other side of the fence. "Leaves in an hour or so. But you'd better go down past them shacks to flip 'er. Us, we aim to head south, maybe to Knoxville."

"Been there," said Stewpot. "If you drop off by the water towers outside of town, there's a jungle there—unless it got busted up, anyways."

"Right. Let's go," one of the men said. He and his companions turned and began walking along the tracks toward the other side of the yard so they could catch a southbound train. Stewpot and Frankie turned to leave as well, but the girl just stood where she was.

One of the men came back and grabbed her roughly by the arm. "Move it, Plain Jane, or we'll leave ya here fer the dogs."

At the mention of dogs, a grimace of fear passed over the

girl's face, and her hand moved to touch the scars on her cheek. Obediently, she turned and walked with the man to join the others.

Frankie watched them, a peculiar feeling in the pit of her stomach. "That girl . . . what's she doing with those men?"

"Same as us," Stewpot replied. "On the drag."

"Why with them?"

"Doesn't know anybody else, I guess," Stewpot said.

"But they aren't very nice to her," protested Frankie.

Stewpot looked grim. "It could be a lot worse for her, Blue. You'll see, frills on the road got it tough—unless they're tough. Even then, they usually find somebody, like those guys, to hang with. Least she's got food this way, and protection."

Who will protect her from *them,* Frankie wondered, but didn't say. "They didn't seem to care about her much. So why do they let her hang with them?" she asked.

Stewpot shifted uncomfortably and stuck his hands in his pockets. "Look, Blue," he said, "there's lots of stuff goes on that isn't very pretty. Let's jest say they get what they want from her, and she gets what she needs from them. Okay? Let's go."

Silently, Frankie followed him to the spot where the other hoboes had suggested waiting for the train to St. Louis. She was thinking about what Stewpot had said. While she didn't understand exactly what he'd meant, the whole incident had made her glad that she had disguised herself as a boy. Mrs. Bailey, it seemed, had been right about the dangers to girls on the road.

Frankie was cold. Inside a shed that blocked the wind, she brushed the snow off some logs that had been cut and piled up, and sat down on them. Stewpot joined her.

Frankie's heart was so full that she was afraid to talk, for fear that she would start to cry in earnest. Stewpot, too, seemed to be in a somber mood. They sat, silent, huddled against the shed, trying to ignore their damp feet and the cold that crept through their clothing.

When the whistle blew and the train appeared in the distance, Frankie got up. She knew that, once again, she was going to have to flip the train, but she was too chilled and downhearted to be scared. Besides, it felt good to move, to know they were *going somewhere*. For the moment, she forced herself not to think about where she was or what she was doing. She tried to think only about the next place, St. Louis, and to make getting there her goal.

The train was moving very slowly, and Frankie jumped on board more easily than the first time, although she still couldn't imagine how Stewpot did it, with no hand waiting to grasp his and pull him up onto the platform. This time, the effort of flipping the train seemed to have tired him. He nodded toward the door handle, and Frankie pulled on it. It opened. As she began to slide the door, she joked halfheartedly, "I hope it's a heated car this time, instead of a reefer, Stew."

Stewpot slid the boxcar door open the rest of the way, and they stepped inside. It was an empty, on its way back to a yard somewhere so it could be loaded again. In the corner was an overturned barrel, and there were some ashes scattered about. Frankie guessed that other hoboes had occupied the empty boxcar before them, and had made a fire in the barrel to stay warm.

"I sure wish we had some firewood," she said with a nod toward the barrel.

"Yeah, or some coal," Stewpot agreed. He spread out his blanket and lay on his back with his hands behind his head. He looked pale and tired. Frankie had noticed that he'd begun coughing from time to time, a deep, hacking cough that shook his whole body. But he managed his usual cheerful grin. "Still, this ain't too bad. At least there wasn't no stew bums or crazies in here already."

Frankie set down her bag and lay beside him on the blanket, using her bag as a headrest. "Hey, what kind of food did that lady give us?" she asked.

"Well," said Stewpot, sitting up and opening the sack. "For *me,* there's buttered biscuits with jam, meat, and cheese. For *you,* let's see, I think there's, yep, one doughnut, hard as a rock—"

Frankie grabbed the bag from his hand. "Give me that!" she said with a laugh.

"Don't tell me you're hungry already after that sit-down we jest had," said Stewpot.

Strangely enough, Frankie *was* hungry. She was always hungry now, it seemed. But she closed the top of the bag and set it aside for later. "I just wanted to know what we had," she said.

The train began to pick up speed, and soon settled into its steady rhythm. The rocking of the car was lulling Frankie to sleep when Stewpot spoke again. "Me and Murph was gonna go partners on the farm. We used to talk about it all the time."

Frankie wanted to ask what happened, but waited. If Stewpot felt like telling her, he would.

"Every 'bo ya meet says he ain't never gonna be a bum. Murph said it all the time. Looked down on the stew bums and tomato-can vags and jungle buzzards, drinkin' rotgut and beggin'. 'Don't they got no self-respect?' he used to say." Stewpot was quiet for a minute, then his voice grew angry. "Then somethin' happened to him. Started hoistin' the booze himself—*Murph*! I couldn't believe it. He laughed when I talked about the farm, said it would never happen. 'They'll never let us get nothin',' he said."

"Who's *they*?" Frankie asked.

Stewpot shrugged. "I dunno exactly. When he was drunk, he'd get ravin' about '*them.*' Thought all the swells and all the stiffs in politics and jest about everybody who wasn't a bum was against him. Said fer the likes of us, it's always gonna be hard times."

"Where is he now?" Frankie asked softly.

Stewpot didn't answer for a long time, and when he did he spoke in a voice filled with pain and bewilderment. "He drowned in his own puke in a flophouse in Detroit."

A gasp of horror escaped before Frankie could stop it. "I'm sorry," she whispered.

They rode for a while in silence. Stewpot had told Frankie about Murph and that made her feel good; it made her want to confide in him, too. She didn't want to pretend any longer to be someone she wasn't. It didn't feel right to be keeping such a big secret from Stewpot. It felt like lying.

And there was something else. Sitting and talking with Stewpot in the dimly lit boxcar, she felt an aching, yearning feeling inside. She couldn't have said what it was, exactly, that she longed for. All she knew was that she felt closer to Stewpot than she'd ever felt to anyone. She was very much aware that he was a boy, and she wanted him to know she was a girl.

"Stewpot?" she began hesitantly.

"Yeah?"

Frankie decided to start with the easiest part. "I want to tell you something. About me. I—I came from—my father was—well, he was a swell, I guess. I mean, he was very rich."

To her astonishment, Stewpot merely said, "I figured that."

Frankie was quite taken aback. "How did you know?"

139

"Lotsa things," answered Stewpot.

Frankie was quiet, trying to think of what she had done to give herself away. Probably just about everything, she reflected wryly. She hadn't known *anything* when she first met Stewpot. It seemed like a lifetime ago.

"You said your father *was* rich," Stewpot said, and waited. "Did he go broke?"

"Yes," Frankie answered. She took a deep breath. "And then he—he . . ." She faltered. "He shot himself."

Stewpot whistled under his breath. "That's tough luck, Blue," he said sympathetically.

"There's another thing I want to tell you," Frankie said, then paused. Stewpot looked at her, interested but not pushing. "I . . ." She stopped again. *Just say it,* she told herself. "Well, the thing is," she began. Then, anxious to have it out and get it over with, she blurted, "I'm a girl! I mean, a frill."

She waited, her whole body stiff with tension, for Stewpot's reaction. Would he be angry with her for deceiving him? Would he throw her off the train in disgust? No, she thought, Stewpot wouldn't do that. But as soon as they stopped, he'd get away from her just as quickly as he could—and if that happened, she didn't think she could bear it.

All Stewpot said was "I figured that, too."

"What?" Frankie exploded. *"You knew I was a girl?"*

Stewpot nodded, looking amused.

"*How* did you know?" Frankie demanded. "*When* did you know?" She could feel her face flushing a deep red, and was hoping that Stewpot couldn't tell.

"First day out," said Stewpot, barely able to control his grin.

"You did not! How did you—you—" Frankie stopped sputtering and got control of herself. "How did you know?" she asked calmly.

"Well, for one thing," said Stewpot, "when we bunked in the jungle, ya gave me somethin' to put under my head. In the morning, when I got a good look at it, it sure wasn't nothin' a guy would wear."

Thinking back, Frankie remembered. Stupid, stupid, stupid, she thought. He'd probably spotted the blouse and pinafore and stockings in her bag countless other times, as well; she'd never remembered to throw them out.

"There was other stuff, too. Like when we was swimmin'. I mean, who swims in their Skivvies? And the way ya was goin' in the bushes all the time . . . and that stuff that Omaha Red lifted off ya, brushes and combs and all . . . and jest the way ya talk, ya know? I'd have to be deaf, dumb, blind, and stupid not to know ya was a frill."

"What about the way I talk?" Frankie asked, feeling foolish now, and defensive. Sure, maybe sometimes she'd forgotten to deepen her voice, but still . . .

"You know . . ." Stewpot hedged.

"No," said Frankie, "I don't. What's the matter with the way I talk?"

"Nothin's the matter," Stewpot said quickly. "It's jest that . . . well . . ." His voice grew low, as if *he* were embarrassed. "Sometimes ya say nice things, frilly things. Ya know what I mean?"

Frankie puzzled over that. Finally she asked, "Don't boys say nice things?"

"A guy might think somethin', but he wouldn't say it, ya know? Makes him sound like a sissy."

"Oh," said Frankie, not sure she knew what he meant. But before she could figure it out, a new thought struck her. "Did everybody know? Vera and Dot, and Blink, and Al . . . and everybody else we've met?"

"Naw," said Stewpot. "You're doin' fine. It's jest that we've been, ya know, spendin' so much time together."

Still smarting at having been found out, Frankie didn't answer. She wasn't sure Stewpot was right that she had fooled the others. Maybe he was just saying that to make her feel better.

Stewpot added offhandedly, "And I gotta say: you're pretty swell fer a frill, Blue. Ya got guts."

Frankie blushed all over again, this time with pleasure. Stewpot had known all along she was a girl and he liked her anyway. He said she had *guts*. She thought it was the finest compliment she'd ever been given.

142

"So, Frankie Blue," Stewpot went on, "what was yer name when ya was a swell?"

"Frances Barrow. Frances *Elizabeth* Barrow. But there was a man—" She stopped as a lump formed in her throat at the thought of Junius. "He called me Frankie."

Stewpot doffed his cap. "James Haskell here. Pleased to meetcha, Frances Elizabeth Barrow." Then he added, as if he were remembering something long forgotten, "My ma called me Jamie sometimes."

Frankie looked at Stewpot, trying to see him as Jamie Haskell. It wasn't easy: He was *Stewpot.* "Your ma," she asked carefully, "do you ever see her?"

"Naw, I can't go back there. My old man'd use me fer a punchin' bag, then he'd start in on her."

Stewpot's words made Frankie's stomach flip-flop. She thought back to what Blink had said about Vera's home life, and Dot's. They had run away to save themselves from things Frankie could never have imagined just a week ago. She thought about her father. She had often been afraid of disappointing him, but she had never feared that he would hit her.

Was it hard times that had made Stewpot's and Dot's fathers, and Vera's mother's boyfriend, cruel and violent? No, she decided, that couldn't be it. Lots of people suffered mean circumstances without becoming mean themselves. Stewpot, for instance. And Peg-Leg Al and Blink. They just kept going somehow, despite their hard times and their injuries. Vera and Dot had tried to leave their troubles behind and go on.

And then there was her father, who, faced with difficult times, had chosen *not* to go on.

"Stew," she said, "when Murph died, were you mad?"

Stewpot looked surprised. "At who?"

"At him."

Stewpot thought for a moment. "It sounds funny when ya say it like that, but, yeah, I guess I was. 'Cause he was my partner, ya know? And how could he do that to me?"

Frankie nodded.

"But that was jest me feelin' sorry fer myself. I got over that pretty quick, and ya know what I began to wonder?"

Frankie shook her head.

"What was hurtin' him so bad he had to go do that to hisself?"

Frankie didn't answer. She was thinking about what Stewpot had said. Murph had killed himself slowly, with booze. Her father's method was faster, but the result was the same. Stewpot's question was a good one.

"Ya think ya know a guy, and—" Stewpot broke off with a shrug.

Frankie pictured her father, alone in his room with a gun and a despair so great he couldn't see past it. The anger she had felt for him began to ease, and in its place was an immense sorrow. She was sorry that he had felt such hopelessness, and sad to think she had never really known him.

144

"I'm gonna get a little shut-eye, Blue," Stewpot murmured. Frankie saw that his eyes were already closed. "Ya been kinda stingy with that harmonica lately: how 'bout it?"

She had almost forgotten about her harmonica. She took it out of her pocket and began to play. As she played, she thought about her father, and Murph, and hoped that, wherever they were, they had found some peace. She thought about Stewpot, and how he'd known all along that she was a girl. When she remembered all the small acts of kindness he had shown her over the past four days, she wondered if he'd have treated her differently if he'd thought she was a boy.

She glanced at him, thinking she might ask, and saw that he was sleeping. Looking at his pale, freckled face, her heart swelled with affection and gratitude. He knew she was a girl—and he thought she was *swell*. She curled up beside him and soon was fast asleep herself.

They were both still sleeping when the train came to a stop in the yard in St. Louis.

"Guess we'll have to take our chances the bulls won't spot us," Stewpot said.

Frankie cautiously slid the door a few inches to the side, and peered out. Stewpot joined her, looked around, and shrugged. "Let's go."

Frankie jumped out first. As she waited for Stewpot to join her, she heard a voice shout, "You there! You're under arrest!"

Eighteen

$\mathcal{F}$rankie and Stewpot were rounded up, along with thirteen other hoboes, and handed over by the railroad bulls to the local police. Most of the tramps surrendered resignedly, as if this had happened to them many times before and would happen many times again.

One young man held back, saying, "I ain't goin' nowhere," and when the police assured him that he was, indeed, going to jail, he snarled, "Try and make me."

Before Frankie realized what was happening, the policeman's nightstick was in his hand, and the young man lay on the ground, stunned by a blow to the shoulder. Two of the other 'boes helped him up, and they began to walk to the

146

station house. One policeman led the procession, and the other brought up the rear, with Frankie and the rest of the hoboes in between.

Frankie could hardly believe what was happening. She walked with her head down, sick with shame at being arrested and taken to jail, and was glad that this was something her father would never know about.

She felt as if the eyes of every passerby must be on her, but when she looked up she was surprised to see that most people averted their eyes or gazed at the little parade without emotion. She supposed they were used to seeing hoboes rounded up, and that it was a sight they preferred not to dwell on.

They passed a girl about Frankie's own age, who was walking with her little brother. The girl said loudly, "Bums. Say 'bums,' Donald. Dirty bums." The girl's casual heartlessness made Frankie's shame turn to anger. She wanted to shout, "You think you're better than we are? Well, you're not!" But what good would that do? It might earn her a blow to the head.

She stole a glance at Stewpot. Her anger was overcome by worry when she saw how tired and dispirited and ill he suddenly looked.

At the station, they were taken to the basement. The policeman pointed to two tin washbasins and said, "Clean yourselves up now." He stood, waiting, as they took turns washing. The water was cold; the soap was harsh and smelled unpleasant and burned Frankie's hands as she scrubbed. When she looked for something to dry off with, the policeman nodded toward a pile of old newspapers.

The hoboes were told to crowd into the only two empty cells. "You'll get dinner and breakfast," the policeman announced. "In the morning, I want you all on the first train out of town, understand?" No one answered, but no one argued, either.

A while later, the policeman and two women served the meal: a cup of cold tomatoes, mostly juice, one cold boiled potato still in its scabby skin, and a slice of sour bread. As they ate, Frankie noticed that the common criminals in the other jail cells were given large bowls of thick, hot stew, fresh bread, mashed potatoes, a dish of prunes, coffee, and cake. She'd heard one of them bragging about his crimes, a string of robberies that ended when he was caught after assaulting an elderly shopkeeper.

It seemed unfair to her that she and Stewpot, who had done nothing but ride in an empty boxcar, were sitting on the cold cement floor with food that was barely fit to eat, while five criminals enjoyed mattresses, blankets, and good, hot food in their cells. She wanted to say something about it to Stewpot, but felt uncomfortable talking in front of so many strangers.

The young man who had been clubbed with the nightstick suddenly threw his cup of tomatoes against the wall, hollering, "You think I'm gonna eat this swill?"

One of the lawbreakers called from his cell, "Ya damn ungrateful bum. Ya oughtta be thankful ya got anything at all."

At that, a loud argument broke out, with the hoboes and the jailed men shouting curses and insults back and forth. Frankie was frightened by the uproar, and by the anger that seemed to spiral out of nowhere. She looked at Stewpot, who was keeping his head down and his mouth shut. She did the same.

A different policeman appeared in the corridor, frowning and swinging his nightstick from side to side. He boomed, "Knock it off, all of you."

The angry young man muttered something Frankie couldn't hear.

"Shut your face," the policeman commanded, "or I'll shut it for you."

There was an uneasy silence. "Now keep it that way," the policeman warned. "Don't make me tell you again." He turned to leave.

Frankie spoke, the words coming out before she even knew she was going to say them. "Excuse me, sir, but my friend isn't feeling so well. Is there a doctor here?"

Stewpot looked up, startled. "Quiet, Blue," he said in a low voice. "I'm fine."

The policeman turned back, a look of amusement on his face. "What do you think this is, kid? A hospital?" He walked toward the stairs, laughing and shaking his head, muttering, "A doctor. That's a good one."

Frankie could feel her lip starting to tremble, and she bit down on it, hard, to keep from crying. Her feelings were such a jumble of humiliation, anger, misery, and worry over Stewpot that she found it almost impossible to control herself. But all she and Stewpot needed now was for her to cry, and for all these men to discover she was a girl. She didn't know why the idea of that seemed dangerous, exactly, but it did.

"It's okay, Blue," Stewpot said quietly. "I just need to pound my ear fer a coupla hours, be good as new."

His face was drawn and pale, and Frankie could feel the effort it took for him to smile. "Sure, Stew," she said.

To Frankie, the night seemed endless. One of the men in the cell was moaning and shouting in his sleep; Stewpot explained that he was "coming out of a drunk." Others snored and snorted; some coughed along with Stewpot. The smell of their unwashed bodies filled her nostrils. Unable to get comfortable on the hard cement floor, she sat, eyes open, as the cell grew dark and the hours of the night crept slowly by.

When morning finally came, they were served a cup of watery cornmeal mush poured into last night's unwashed tin bowl, and another slice of stale bread. Frankie was too downhearted to care that the criminals in their single cells were given eggs with bacon, toast, oatmeal, and coffee.

After the hoboes had eaten, they were escorted back to the railroad tracks, where they were told to hop the next train out of town and not come back. They weren't allowed to hit the street to get food for the journey, nor were they permitted to board a train in the yard. The policemen waited, grim-faced, to see that they did, in fact, jump on the train as it went by.

This time, it was Frankie who climbed aboard first. Stewpot was too weak to make it alone, and she gave him a hand up. The car was full of crates, stacked one on top of the other. They scrambled to the top of the pile and sat, panting, in the dark.

"It doesn't make sense," Frankie said. "First we get arrested for hopping a train. Then they make us hop another just to get rid of us."

"Nobody cares what happens to 'boes, Blue, as long as we keep on movin' to someplace else." He coughed and spat, then added, "At least this train's goin' in the right direction."

 *Nineteen*

*O*utside of Davenport, Iowa, Frankie and Stewpot dropped off the train and walked into town. Frankie was starving after the long trip without food. Stewpot had wanted to hit the stem and then find the nearest jungle, but Frankie was sure that he needed some rest. He had mentioned that there was a mission in town. Knowing he would protest going there, she pretended that it was she who was tired and cold.

"Hey, Stew? I sure would like to spend just one night in a warm place where we can get some food without having to work for it. Can we go to that mission you told me about—just for tonight?"

It took some persuading, but Stewpot finally agreed. "Okay. We'll hit the flophouse for one night," he said, "but then we're gonna keep goin', like we said we was gonna do. I aim to see if Murph was right about how pretty them Rocky Mountains are."

He pointed ahead to a run-down–looking building and said, "There she is." As they drew closer, Frankie became apprehensive. She didn't know what to expect, never having been to a mission before. Stewpot had painted a grim picture, but, still, she hoped it would be a nice, warm place where he could get a good night's sleep, some nourishing, hot food, and perhaps some medicine for his cold.

She was disappointed to find that in many ways the mission was a lot like jail, except that, for the most part, the mission workers were nicer than the police. Signs were posted all about. Most had quotes from the Bible printed on them. "It's Never Too Late for Jesus," read one. "When Did You Last Write Home to Mother?" asked another. On a bench in a corner, a mission worker read monotonously from a book. No one appeared to be listening. Frankie caught only the words "Renounce your sins and be saved" before Stewpot motioned for her to join him in front of a counter on the other side of the room.

There, she and Stewpot were registered and given a ticket with a number on it. Then all the newcomers were told to separate, men in one line and women in another.

Frankie looked at Stewpot with alarm. "What should I do?"

"Looks like they're gonna make us strip," he said, "so ya gotta go with the frills. It's okay. I'll meet up with ya after."

Nervously, Frankie joined several other girls and women. She looked back over her shoulder at Stewpot, who was disappearing along with a much larger group of men. Frankie and the other women were led to a room where they were told to remove their clothing for fumigation. Then they were taken to an open bathroom to shower and wait for their clothing to be returned.

The water was cold. Frankie washed quickly, then sat on the cement floor, trying her best to cover up with the small, rough towel she had been given. She was anxious about being separated from Stewpot, and wanted her clothes back so she could join him again.

Snatches of talk from the other girls and women swirled around her.

"So the switchman says to me, 'Come on in here with me, girlie, and warm yourself,' and I says, 'Warm your own self.'"

". . . train pulled me and dragged the soles right off my shoes."

"I told him I'd run away if he didn't ease up with the belt. 'Go ahead,' he said. 'You'll be back for supper.' Guess I showed him."

"I don't know what that stuff was I was drinking, but I was sicker than a dog the next morning."

"It helps to wear a skirt on the main stem when you're giving your spiel, but you'll freeze your tail in a boxcar."

"I got tobacco to trade if anybody has some socks that don't got holes in 'em."

". . . and when he found out I was gonna have a baby, he told me to hit the road."

Frankie shivered and pulled the towel closer. To her relief, her clothes were soon returned. She put them on and went to the main hall, which was filled with makeshift tables and chairs. There she found Stewpot, also freshly bathed.

They lined up with the other tramps to receive their food: thin, watery oatmeal in shallow tin dishes, with a slice of dry bread on top. It was not a tantalizing sight, but Frankie couldn't wait to eat.

She followed Stewpot to a table where there were two seats left. She sat next to an old man wearing a tattered overcoat, a wool watch cap pulled down over his forehead, and gloves with the fingers missing. He was hunched over his food with one arm held protectively around the dish. The other hand moved quickly, shoveling gruel into his mouth. He looked up briefly, his eyes narrow with suspicion, and Frankie saw that his long gray whiskers were flecked with bits of his dinner.

She turned away quickly, set down her plate, and looked at Stewpot. "You don't look half bad with a clean face, Stew," she teased. He poked her in return, and when she looked back at her plate, the slice of bread was gone.

The old man next to her was hunched over his plate again, chewing quickly, his cheeks bulging—with her bread! His sly, furtive movements made her think of a wild creature—a rat, perhaps, or a ferret. There was something about his cunning, silent desperation that frightened her. Afraid to say anything, she merely sat where she was.

A woman she recognized from the shower let out a cackle. Giving Frankie a sly wink, the woman said, "Learned somethin', didn't ya?" She cackled again, her mouth a dark cavern that held just three broken teeth.

Frankie looked down and ate her gruel quickly. Stewpot had warned her not to expect seconds, and she had no intention of calling attention to her thieving dinner companion by asking for another piece of bread. She wanted only to get away from the table as soon as possible.

Stewpot offered her his bowl, saying he wasn't hungry. Frankie looked at him, astonished: Stewpot, not hungry? The last he'd eaten was the poor fare they'd been given in jail.

"You've got to eat, Stewpot, if you're going to get well," she said.

"Grub like this'll *make* ya sick if ya ain't already," Stewpot grumbled.

"Please?" Frankie whispered and, to her relief, Stewpot began, unenthusiastically, to eat. When he had finished, Frankie asked, "What do we do now?"

"Claim us a bunk," Stewpot said with a shrug.

156

Upstairs, all the cots were taken, so Frankie and Stewpot found an open area on the floor as far as possible from the stinking bathroom that occupied the other end of the room. The smell from the overworked toilet mingled with the disinfectant odor that clung to everyone's clothing. Frankie held her hand over her nose and mouth, but it didn't help.

From below, Frankie heard the beginning of a hymn being played on the piano. For a moment, she thrilled at the familiar sound. Then she winced: the piano was badly out of tune, and was being pounded with a heavy hand. At the sound, the other tramps began shuffling reluctantly down the stairs.

"Time for angel food," said Stewpot, giving Frankie a wink. At her puzzled look, he explained, "Now we get the sermon. Gotta stand up for Jesus if you want a meal and a place to flop."

Frankie and Stewpot joined the others on benches facing the piano-playing preacher and sang,

"I need Jesus, I need Jesus.
Every day along the way,
Yes, I need Jesus."

Behind Frankie, a voice muttered, "What *I* need is a new pair of pants."

"I need me a drink," said another.

The preacher intoned, "I now call on the Lord to witness and on the assembled to declare your faith in Jesus."

There was a long silence, and Frankie began to squirm on the hard wooden bench. Finally a man rose and said, "I ain't got much, but what I got, the Lord gave it to me. What did the Devil ever give to me? Nothin', that's what!" He sat down, to the preacher's enthusiastic "Amen."

A few others followed, including one drunken man who swayed, stared about blankly, mumbled something no one could understand, and sat down.

This sad gathering was nothing like the church services Frankie was used to attending, and she soon gave up trying to keep her eyes open. She must have dozed, because she was awakened by the sound of the piano playing the closing hymn.

She and Stewpot filed up the stairs with the others. Stewpot slept fitfully, awakened by his own coughing and congestion. Frankie, now that she had "earned" her night's rest, was unable to sleep. She stared, wide-eyed and miserable, into the darkness. She thought about the night she and Stewpot spent in the jungle in Pittsburgh, and how exciting it had been to sleep out under the stars, how safe and happy she had felt. But now, several long days later, she was tired and hungry and scared and homesick.

She thought about the other women's conversations in the shower room. Their talk had made her feel uncomfortable. Worse, she felt childish and spoiled. What would they have said, she wondered, if she had told them she was on the street because she didn't want to live in Chicago with her aunt. That she didn't want to live in a warm house where she'd have her own soft bed, and her own clean bathroom, and plenty of good, hot food. That she didn't want to live in a safe place where no one would dream of raising a hand to her. That she just wanted to be "free as the wind."

She let out a hollow laugh, imagining the looks of amazement on their hard, tired faces. Bughouse, they'd call her, crippled under the hat. And wouldn't they be right?

Twenty

_I_n the morning there was more of the same thin, watery gruel, and another slice of bread. This time, Frankie leaned over her food and didn't take her eyes off it until she had finished.

"Stewpot," she whispered when they had pushed their plates away. She still felt uneasy speaking with so many ears listening. "What do we do now?"

"Any of these stiffs who wants to stay gets put to work now," he said. "But you and me are takin' off."

Frankie was relieved to hear him say they were leaving. She hated the mission, with its close, cramped quarters, foul odors, and air of hopelessness. "But where will we go?" she asked.

"Like we said. To Montana."

"Stew, do you think . . ." She paused, not sure how to say what she wanted to ask. "Are you sure?"

Stewpot's jaw was set. "I'm sure about one thing, Blue: I ain't stayin' one more night in this stinkin' hole. All I know is I gotta move, breathe some fresh air quick."

"Stew," said Frankie, "I was thinking last night. And, well, I have an aunt who lives in Chicago. We could go there. Both of us. And—"

"An aunt in Chicago? So that's who you was runnin' from." He paused, then said, "You go." His eyes were serious.

"What about you?" Frankie asked.

Stewpot smiled at her gently. "I don't think so, Blue. Ya think yer aunt would be happy to see the likes of me at the door?"

Frankie faltered. It was a good question. She didn't even know if *she* would be welcome, after she had run away without a word. "She'll like you once she gets to know you," Frankie said, not at all sure this was true.

"Look, Blue," said Stewpot, "you know how to act around swells, but me, I ain't suited to it. I'm gonna get me that farm, remember? And, in the meantime, I aim to see them mountains."

They were quiet for a moment. Then Stewpot said, "Y'oughtta go, Blue, I ain't kiddin'. What d'ya aim to do, stay on the drag forever?"

"How about coming with me just until you're better?" Frankie begged.

"Naw, I'll be fine as soon as I kick this cough. Besides, I came this far. I'm gonna see them Rockies."

"Well, then, I'm going with you," Frankie declared. That settled the matter for the moment. When Stewpot tried to protest again, she silenced him with a look. She couldn't imagine leaving him now, not when he was sick. When he was well again, then she'd think about what to do next. Maybe after Stewpot saw the mountains, he'd be willing to go to Chicago with her, at least until the hard times were over.

"You stay here while I find the main stem and get us some grub for the trip," she said.

Stewpot began to protest, but Frankie shushed him with a look. "You think I can't hit the street by myself?" she challenged.

When Stewpot hesitated, she pressed her advantage. "While I'm gone, you talk to these stiffs and find out what train we want and what the situation is with the bulls."

"Geez," said Stewpot, "you're gettin' as bossy as that Vera." But he was grinning when he said it, and Frankie grinned back, feeling an odd pleasure at giving the orders for a change.

Frankie found the main section of town without difficulty. Within a couple of hours, she had managed to secure three loaves of day-old bread, five carrots, three apples that were just a bit shriveled, and a stick of greasy, spicy salami that didn't smell spoiled at all.

When she returned triumphantly to the mission, she found a scowling Stewpot washing dishes. "I was here, so I got stuck pearl diving," he said. "I might as well stay for lunch, seein' as I earned it."

Frankie ate a piece of the bread she had begged, while Stewpot had his bowl of watery soup. Then Stewpot turned in his bowl, and they stepped out together into the crisp, cold afternoon.

They approached the yard cautiously and watched for a while. Seeing no bulls patrolling, they found an opening in the fence and sneaked through. They walked along the lines of cars, checking waybills, until they found a freighter going their way, then climbed inside to wait.

When they were settled in, Frankie asked, "What's in Seattle, anyway?"

"Some guys at the mission said there's a Hooverville there. Said we can stay there as long as we want."

"A Hooverville?" Frankie repeated. "What's that?"

"Ain't ya never heard that before?" Stewpot asked. "It's like a little town set up by people who got nowhere else to go. There's plenty of 'em, all over the country. They're named after our high and mighty President, who don't give

163

a rat's tail about people like us. Folks make shacks outta whatever they can scrounge up, plant themselves, and stick around."

"Is it like a jungle?" Frankie asked.

"Sorta, only jungles are for guys on the move, like us. And cops can come and bust up a jungle. These Hoovervilles get so big that after a while there ain't nobody dares try to mess with 'em. There's whole families livin' there, from what I hear, little babies and kids and stuff."

Frankie tried to imagine it.

"We can take a look, anyways. If we don't like it, we'll leave," Stewpot said with a shrug. Then, grinning sardonically, he asked, "Ya know what a Hoover blanket is?"

Frankie shook her head.

"A newspaper. How 'bout a Hoover flag?"

Again, Frankie shook her head.

"A guy's empty pockets turned inside out and flappin' in the breeze." Stewpot laughed, but Frankie didn't think the jokes were funny. They seemed to her to hide a bitter despair. Did President Hoover know of these "towns" named after him? And if so, wasn't there something he could do to help the people there? These were new thoughts for Frankie, and they occupied her mind as the train moved north and Stewpot slept.

The hours crawled by. They rode for two days, traveling through St. Paul and stopping briefly in Fargo. Their food ran out, and by the time they arrived in Grand Forks,

Frankie was hungrier than she'd ever been in her life—and colder.

Looking out at the bleak, bare, windswept landscape of the North Dakota winter, she experienced a deep foreboding. For a moment, she had the frightening sensation that she and Stewpot were the only people left on a cold, indifferent planet. She felt lost, with no sense of where they were. She was almost glad to see a guard patrolling the yard, swinging his nightstick, his breath making big white clouds in the frosty air.

When he was out of sight, she and Stewpot jumped down from the boxcar and ran to the safety of an abandoned freight shack. Shaking off her dreary thoughts, Frankie helped Stewpot build a little fire, then said, "I'm going into town for some grub."

Stewpot began to rise from his place by the fire.

"You stay," said Frankie quickly. "There's no sense in both of us going and, this way, you can keep watch on what's happening in the yard."

It was a lame excuse, and she and Stewpot both knew it. She held her breath, hoping he would agree to stay where he could rest and stay warm.

"Okay, Blue," he said finally.

The sun was already beginning to go down, marking the end of the short winter day, as Frankie made her way carefully and stealthily across the yard. Stewpot had said he thought they had a couple of hours before the train would be ready to depart; it was enough time for what she planned to do.

Stewpot hadn't wanted her to spend any of her money, telling her to save it for a time when things got rough. She didn't know if he'd agree that this was the time, and she didn't care.

Frankie walked until she found a small grocery store. Passing the window, she saw a thin, dirty-faced boy with a tense, pale face and was startled to realize it was her own reflection. Inside, she bought two loaves of bread, two quarts of milk, four apples, a chunk of cheese, some canned meat, and four cans of beans. She piled them on the counter, and went back for a can opener and a small tin cooking pot.

After paying, she carefully placed the change back inside her shoe, ignoring the staring eyes of the clerk. Carrying the sack of food, she followed the grocer's directions to a dry goods store, where she purchased two blankets, two wool watch caps, and two pairs of wool gloves. Then she went to a drugstore and asked the man behind the counter what medicine he would suggest for a person with a bad cold.

The pharmacist asked a few questions, which Frankie answered. Yes, fatigue and weakness. Yes, coughing, congestion, sore throat. Fever? She didn't know. The man turned behind him to the shelves filled with bottles and tins and jars.

"This should help ease the coughing a bit. And this aspirin can work wonders, especially if your friend gets feverish. But it's no substitute for bed rest, warmth, good hot food, and plenty of liquids. Do you understand?"

Miserably, Frankie nodded. "How much is the medicine?" she asked.

"The small bottle is forty-nine cents; the large is eighty-nine cents."

"I'll take two of the large ones," Frankie said, bending down once again to untie her shoe.

"Follow the directions on the label," the man advised. "It'll probably make him sleepy, but that's for the best."

When Frankie turned to leave, he said gently, "Good luck to you, son. And your friend."

Frankie murmured her thanks and fled before the pharmacist could see the tears that suddenly flooded her eyes. The bags, one heavy and one bulky, slowed her steps, but her thoughts were racing: Would two bottles last long enough to get them across the Rocky Mountains to Seattle? Should she have bought three bottles instead? Was Hooverville a place where Stewpot could rest and get well? Would there be hot food, like the mulligan in the jungle? Would the blankets and the hat and the gloves be enough to keep him warm?

She calculated the amount of money she had left: forty-four dollars and sixty-five cents. She wondered if it was enough to pay for a hospital or a doctor if Stewpot got sicker. She felt sick herself at all the questions for which she had no answers.

_____ *Twenty-one*

*W*hen Frankie returned to the shack, Stewpot woke up. "What ya got in them bags?" he asked sleepily. Frankie just smiled. "Come on," she said. "Let's find us a car and get settled. Then I'll show you."

They crept down the line, peering into the cars. One was full of coal dust, and from another came a drunken warning, "This here's taken." Finally Frankie called excitedly to Stewpot. "Here's one, and it's got a barrel in it. Let's get some stuff to make a fire."

Frankie went back to the coal car to gather as many stray pieces of coal as she could carry. Stewpot returned with some empty wooden crates, which they hauled into the

168

boxcar and broke up with their feet. When a small blaze was burning, they sat down close to its warmth.

"Nice," said Frankie.

"Now, ya gonna show me what's in them bags?" Stewpot asked. He was amazed when Frankie produced the food, warm clothing, blankets, and medicine. "I don't guess you need me no more, Blue. You're a real blowed-in-the-glass stiff!"

Then he took a good look at the grocery sack and the brand-new clothes and blankets and said quietly, "I told ya to save yer dough, Blue."

"Don't be mad, Stew," she pleaded. "You said I'd need it if something happened to you. And I'm just making sure nothing *does* happen."

"Aw, Blue, I ain't mad," Stewpot said. "This stuff is swell. I jest wanted you to hang on to yer money fer a rainy day, ya know?"

"Well, that's what I did," Frankie said firmly. Then, grinning, she added, "So go ahead and take your medicine like a good boy."

Stewpot smiled faintly, but seemed to have something else on his mind. He looked at her and said quietly, "Ya know, Blue, before you came along, there were times I was so lonely I wanted to howl like a dern dog. If I was on my own right now, feelin' so lousy and all, well . . ." He gave a short, embarrassed laugh, then looked away.

Frankie listened, glad that she hadn't left Stewpot when

169

he needed her. His words, more than the wool cap on her head and the gloves on her hands, warmed her through and through. She wanted to tell Stewpot that, but didn't know how. Instead she joked, "That's real nice, Stew, but it's not going to get you out of taking your medicine." She handed him one of the bottles. "Here. The man at the store said to follow the directions on the label."

Stewpot stared at the bottle with something close to panic in his eyes. There was a long pause. "So I jest swig some?" he said finally.

"How much does it say to take?" Frankie asked.

"I dunno," said Stewpot. In a voice that was barely audible, he added, "I—well, I don't read so good."

"Oh," said Frankie softly. She thought about the night she had tried to offer Stewpot a book to read. She felt stupid for not having figured out why he'd refused, and for embarrassing him unnecessarily over the medicine label.

Taking the bottle, she read the directions to herself, then handed it back. "Take a tablespoon every two hours or whenever you start to cough."

Stewpot nodded, but didn't move to take the medicine. He sat gazing at the barrel, almost as if he were watching the flames that burned inside.

"It's funny," Frankie said carefully. "I had a secret, and you did, too."

"Funny, yeah," said Stewpot. "But it's not so funny when people laugh at ya and say you're dumb."

170

Frankie was filled with indignation at the idea of anyone saying Stewpot was dumb. He was one of the smartest people she'd ever known. If he wasn't, he'd never have survived on the road for three years, she was sure of that.

She had a sudden idea. "Stewpot!" she said excitedly. "I'll teach you to read!"

"I dunno, Blue," Stewpot said reluctantly. "Teacher said once there's somethin' wrong with me, with my brain."

"That's the most ridiculous thing I ever heard of!" said Frankie furiously. "There is nothing wrong with your brain! That teacher's the one who's stupid!"

"Okay, okay, Blue," Stewpot said with a faint chuckle. "Take it easy." He reached for the bottle and cautiously took a drink of the medicine.

"Cripes," he said, shuddering at the taste. "Stuff that nasty has got to either cure ya or croak ya."

Frankie smiled. Watching Stewpot take his medicine made her feel good inside, and hopeful. They ate quietly for a while. Then Stewpot began to grow drowsy, as the man in the store had said he might. "I think I'm gonna cop a little snooze," he murmured, and snuggled down beneath the blanket.

As the train moved steadily westward and Stewpot slept, Frankie tried to remember how Miss Chenier had taught *her* to read. It was hard to think back that far, and impossible to recall a time when she had *not* been able to read. But she could teach Stewpot, she knew she could. It would be something she could do to pay him back for all that he had taught her.

At some point, she must have fallen asleep, because she was startled into wakefulness by a rattling sound. Looking at Stewpot, she saw he was shivering so violently that his boots were banging against the boxcar floor. She was afraid his chattering teeth might break. Worst of all was the look of pain and fear in his eyes.

"Stew!" she gasped. "What's wrong?"

"C-c-c-cold," Stewpot managed to say.

Quickly Frankie untangled herself from her blanket and wrapped it around Stewpot. She got up and checked the barrel. The fire had burned itself out; she started it again, her own hands trembling. The boxcar was cold, but they had slept through worse. She knew that Stewpot's bone-shaking chill was not from the temperature in the car. It meant that he was very sick.

The next minute, Stewpot began moaning and thrashing about and throwing off the blankets. Frankie felt his forehead, the way Mrs. Bailey had always done when she suspected fever, and pulled her hand back in alarm. Stewpot was burning up, his skin hot and clammy with sweat.

Remembering the pharmacist's advice, Frankie managed to poke two of the aspirin between Stewpot's chattering teeth and make him swallow them. Then, not knowing what else to do, she lay down beside him and wrapped her arms around him, trying to will the warmth from her body into his. After what seemed a long time, she felt the shivering subside and she almost cried with relief.

The hours passed slowly. Frankie felt more alone and frightened than ever before in her life, and utterly helpless. She did the only things she could think of, urging Stewpot to drink more medicine and take more aspirin. She talked soothingly about his farm and about teaching him to read. Silently, she prayed.

At last the hectic fits of fever passed, leaving Stewpot exhausted and quiet. He slept, and Frankie, curled beside him, slept, too.

Twenty-two

$\mathcal{F}$rankie awoke when the train began to slow. It was the second day since they'd left Grand Forks, she was pretty sure, but the nightmarish hours of Stewpot's crisis had made the journey seem much longer. Before that, there had been several stops for loading and unloading, when she and Stewpot had slipped out of the car for a "stretch," as he liked to call their trips to the bushes, but by now she had lost track of where they were. Carefully, she slid the boxcar door open slightly so that she could read the station sign as they passed by.

"Havre, Montana, Stew," she said aloud. "But I don't see

174

any mountains. I don't see much of anything at all, just lots and lots of snow and open space."

She was relieved when Stewpot answered, even though his voice was weak. "I told ya the West is big, remember?"

"But where are the Rocky Mountains?"

"Murph said they kinda pop up outta nowhere. We'll know when we get there, 'cause the train's gotta stop and get another engine to help push it. That's how steep and high them Rocky Mountains are!" Stewpot seemed to perk up, just thinking about the Rockies. "Even if I'm poundin' my ear like a baby, you wake me up when we get there. Ya promise, Blue?"

"I promise."

"We'll wrap ourselves up real good in these blankets, open up the door and feast our eyes on the prettiest sight on earth, leastways according to Murph."

Stewpot was well into the second bottle of medicine. After more coughing and another swig from the bottle, he fell back to sleep. Frankie lay awake, praying that Murph had been telling the truth, that the Rocky Mountains were as splendid as he'd said, and that Stewpot wouldn't be disappointed.

Several hours later, Frankie felt the train starting to slow down, and she nudged Stewpot awake. "I think we're there, Stew. How are you feeling?"

"Okay," he answered. "Open the door and let's have a glim."

Frankie slid the door open a few inches and peered out. Two things happened at once: she let out an exclamation of sheer joy at the incredible beauty before her, and the little hairs on the inside of her nose froze up.

"Oh, Stew," she cried, "look!"

"I would if you'd open the door so I can see somethin' besides yer backside!" he answered.

Frankie opened the door farther, and Stewpot, sitting up now, slid forward and joined her.

"Holy Toledo!" Stewpot stared, his eyes wide, his mouth hanging open. Before them rose the mountains, covered in snow. A river cut through two ridges like a thin silver ribbon. The sky was a color of blue Frankie had never seen before, and the light sparkled on the clean white snow, making Frankie and Stewpot squint and shield their eyes with their hands.

But they could not tear their eyes away. It seemed they could see forever, from one mountain ridge to the one beyond, and to another beyond that. Except for the lonely twin lines of railroad track, there wasn't a sign that humans had ever touched the land. A deep quiet came from the trees and the mountains; even the train was quiet, as it waited for the aid of a second engine.

Frankie and Stewpot looked and looked, and couldn't get enough of looking. Then they heard voices and the clank of couplings as the engine hooked onto the rear of their train. The train began to move again, slowly ascending a pass in the mountains. Frankie closed the door to a mere slit until they were away from the station, then opened it again. She and Stewpot settled themselves on the floor, wrapped themselves in a cocoon of blankets, and watched the scenery go by.

They passed under large shed roofs built into the mountainside to protect the train from avalanches. The tracks followed the valley formed by another river, and as they descended from the pass, the thin silver ribbon became a wide, wild, rushing surge. Huge, ice-covered boulders rose from its waters, and log jams formed from many huge trees looked like tiny piles of toothpicks stacked in its many bends and oxbows.

"Look, Stew," said Frankie, and pointed to a herd of animals in the valley.

"Elk," answered Stewpot. "I think."

On a cliffside covered with blue-green ice, mountain goats were gathered to lick salts and minerals from the frozen runoff. Large birds soared above the peaks. Frankie recognized the white head of the bald eagle but could only guess about the others.

Clouds formed, obscuring the sun, and a gentle snowfall filled the gray sky. The snow thickened, and trees and objects appeared as ghostly blurs behind the hypnotic veil of falling flakes. Still Frankie and Stewpot stared.

The endless miles of forest and mountain and sky made Frankie feel incredibly small and insignificant. At the same time, she felt some of their grandeur within herself. She didn't try to explain any of this to Stewpot; she was sure he understood.

Only when the last shred of light had left the sky did they slide the door closed. They huddled next to the barrel, warming their hands. Stewpot was the first to speak, and his words made Frankie grin: "That Murph knew a thing or two, eh, Blue?"

"Yeah, Stew. He sure did."

Twenty-three

As the train made its way through the mountains, Frankie and Stewpot opened the door whenever they dared, and for as long as they could stand the cold. They passed through West Glacier and Whitefish, Montana, through the northernmost tip of Idaho, and into the state of Washington.

Seeing the Rocky Mountains had brought a temporary lift to Stewpot's spirits, but the frigid temperatures they had exposed themselves to had not helped him one bit. There was a stop in Spokane, during which Frankie got off the train and managed to beg some stale doughnuts from a bakery right near the station.

Stewpot had drunk all the medicine, but Frankie didn't know how long the train would be stopped, and was afraid to take the time to buy more. She consoled herself with the thought that the next city they'd come to was Seattle.

The last leg of the journey seemed to Frankie to take forever. Stewpot's cough was much worse. It seized his entire body in fits that left him clutching his chest and gasping. Though he tried to hide it from her, Frankie was alarmed to see that his handkerchief was covered with rusty-colored stains.

By the time the train reached Seattle, she was exhausted from hunger, thirst, and lack of sleep, and nearly sick herself with anxiety over Stewpot. What frightened her most of all was that he seemed hardly to know her. His eyes had a glazed, empty look. His face looked old and drawn and lifeless, except during his long bouts of coughing, when it contorted with pain.

Frankie had never felt so helpless in her life. There was no question of jumping off the train while it was still moving. Stewpot could barely stand up, let alone land on his feet. They would have to risk getting out in the yard after the train had stopped. Frankie almost hoped they'd be caught and arrested. Surely no jailer could ignore someone as obviously sick as Stewpot was—or could he? She thought about the treatment they had received in the jail in St. Louis, and wasn't sure.

When the train came to a halt, Frankie jumped out of

the boxcar and scouted about quickly. Seeing no one, she hoisted herself back into the car, put her bag and Stewpot's bundle on one shoulder, and helped Stewpot down as best she could. Putting one of his arms around her neck, she told him, "Lean on me, Stew, and try to walk."

Stewpot was shaking, and his legs could barely hold him. He listened to Frankie's encouragement and did as she said: "One step . . . There, that's good, Stewpot, that's good. Now another . . . Good, you're doing fine. Come on, keep going. It's not far."

The last was a lie. Frankie had no idea where the place called Hooverville was. She only knew she had to get there. She didn't think beyond that. Once they were there, *something* would happen, *someone* would help her. She just had to *get there*.

They made their way haltingly out of the yard and onto the deserted streets near the docks. At last they came to a more populated area of town. Frankie asked the first person she saw, a woman walking a small dog, the way to Hooverville. The woman turned and quickly walked away without a word. Next she asked two men dressed in warm overcoats, standing on the street corner, smoking cigarettes and talking.

"Get on the train and go back to where you came from," one of the men suggested.

"Just what we need, more bums," said the other, ignoring Frankie and talking to his companion.

"Walking around drunk in broad daylight," said the first, shaking his head in disgust.

Frankie didn't bother to say that Stewpot was sick, not drunk. The men wouldn't believe her, nor would they care. She just kept walking, asking everyone she saw, ignoring their snubs, and praying she didn't run into a policeman.

Then two boys playing ball pointed toward a side street. "Down there. You can't miss it," they shouted.

Stewpot tried to sit down to rest, but Frankie held him tightly around the waist and begged him to remain standing. If he sat down, she was afraid she'd never get him up again. "It's right up here, Stew, honest. Just a little farther. Please, Stewpot, *please.*"

Ahead, in what had once been a vacant lot, was the Hooverville Stewpot had heard about. When she saw it, Frankie's heart sank. Stewpot had told her what to expect, but somehow she had turned it around in her mind, letting herself picture a real town, a town where people who had no homes could make a home, where everyone shared what they had, as they did in the jungle.

Crammed together were hundreds of dwellings made from every kind of unwanted scrap imaginable. People were living in rusted-out car and truck bodies, piano boxes, shacks fashioned from orange crates, ragged sheets of tin and canvas held together by broomsticks, saplings, junk metal and lumber, string and rope and strips of cloth. Smoke from their wood fires hung in the damp, gray air.

A few children in shabby clothes were playing and shrieking on the edges of the camp. At first, as Frankie drew closer with Stewpot, she saw no adults at all. Then she saw that they were hiding, scuttling away like crabs and peering out from their small, dark lairs. She felt their eyes on her, but no one spoke or called out a greeting.

Frankie stood for a moment, utterly at a loss. Then, setting her mouth in a determined line, she said, "Come on, Stewpot." She began making her way between the sad, sagging structures, hoping only that someone would take pity on her. She felt no anger at the people who looked out from their meager shelters, eyes narrowed with fear and suspicion, or blank with hopelessness and fatigue. They had come to the end, as she had; they had no help to offer.

Finally, Stewpot's knees buckled and Frankie could no longer hold him up. He fell to the ground in a crumpled heap, and Frankie fell beside him, laid her head on his chest, and wept.

Twenty-four

Frankie didn't know how long she and Stewpot had been lying on the ground when she heard a voice.

"What's the problem, boys?"

Frankie felt a hand on the back of her head. For a moment, the voice seemed familiar and her heart lifted. She raised her head—but, no, it wasn't Junius, of course it wasn't Junius. The man staring down at her looked nothing at all like Junius. Even so, Frankie felt relief flood through her at the sight of him.

He reached for her hand and helped her to her feet, then leaned down and scooped Stewpot up as if he were a baby. "Come on," he said.

Dazed, Frankie followed the man through the maze of shacks and smoking fires. He stopped at a structure made, it appeared to Frankie, from the roof of a car set over walls made of boards. Across the doorway hung a rug; the man swept it aside and said with a twisted smile, "Welcome to my humble home."

Frankie stepped past him into the dim room. The man followed her inside, set Stewpot down on a makeshift cot, and lit a small oil lamp. Both Frankie and the man looked at Stewpot, who was panting shallowly, his eyes closed.

"He's pretty sick," the man observed.

Frankie nodded, unable to speak.

"You both could use some hot tea," the man said briskly, rummaging in a corner and coming up with a pot. "Be right back. Oh, the name's Jack. But everybody around here calls me Sawbones, on account of I was once studying to be a doc."

"I'm Frankie Blue, and this is"—Frankie swallowed the sudden lump in her throat—"Stewpot." She rushed on desperately, "Is he going to be all right?"

"Hang on there, Frank. Let me get this pot going, then we'll see what's what."

Frankie waited. After a while, she heard Jack return, and she peeked out the doorway to watch as he stirred the fire to life and hung the pot over it to boil. She joined him by the fire. "Jack," she said hesitantly, "you said you were studying to be a doctor. Can you help Stewpot?"

Jack sighed deeply and shook his head. "I didn't get very far in medical school, Frank. All that responsibility . . . life and death in my hands. It's scary, you know what I mean?"

Frankie did know. At least, she knew what it felt like to have Stewpot nearly dying just three feet away. She pleaded, "You must have learned *something.*"

"Look," said Jack, "I'm telling you, I'm no doctor!" His voice was loud, almost angry. He seemed to make an effort to calm himself, then said quietly, "But it looks like pneumonia." He asked about Stewpot's symptoms and nodded as Frankie recounted them. "Yeah. Sounds like pneumonia, all right."

Frankie had heard of pneumonia, but had never known anyone who'd had it. "He'll get over it, though. Won't he?"

Jack looked uncomfortable. "About half the people who get it do," he said. Then he added, "But your friend's pretty bad off. I don't imagine those nights in the boxcar helped him any."

"Can't we *do* something?"

Jack shrugged. "All you can do is try and keep him warm. Make him drink something, even if he doesn't want to. And—wait."

"*Wait?*" With a gasp of despair, Frankie turned back into the little room and knelt beside Stewpot. Gazing at his pale, still face, she cried, "Stew! Can you hear me? You can't die!" Her voice rose, and she couldn't stop it. "Stew? Stew! Can you hear me? Answer me, *please.*"

186

Stewpot opened his eyes and looked toward Frankie without seeing her. His eyes had a strange, faraway look as he said, almost dreamily, "Them mountains sure are pretty, ain't they?"

Frankie was very frightened. "Stewpot," she begged, "I'm going for help. Don't die, do you hear me, Stew? *Wait for me.*"

A faint smile crossed Stewpot's face. "Look at them mountains," he murmured before closing his eyes.

Frankie watched him with horror. His face looked blue. His lips *were* blue! She leaned down and placed her ear against his chest and listened to his labored breath rattle through his lungs. Grasping his shoulders, she began whispering urgently. "You're going to get well, Stew. I know it. And then . . ." She thought to herself, Then I'm going to Chicago and taking you with me, no matter what you say.

What if she were no longer welcome? Not to mention Stewpot. She pushed the thought away. "I'll beg her on my hands and knees if I have to," she whispered. First she had to get Stewpot well enough to travel.

Jumping up, she pushed past the rug hanging in the doorway and said to Jack, "Watch him for me." Hearing the commanding tone in her voice, she added, "Please. I'll be back as soon as I can."

"Sure you're coming back?" Jack looked at her speculatively. "You're not just ditching him here, are you?"

"Of course I'm coming back!" Frankie said angrily.

Then, remembering that Jack had been the only person to offer help, and that she still needed him, she controlled her impatience. "Look, Jack," she said, "it was real nice of you to help me. I'm going for a doctor. Would you watch him while I'm gone?"

"Weren't you listening? A doctor's only going to tell you the same thing I did." Seeing the stubborn line of Frankie's jaw, Jack's expression changed to a curious mixture of amusement, pity, and admiration. "You really think you're going to get a doctor to come to Bum-Town?" he asked.

"Yes," Frankie answered. She would find a doctor, and pay him, and he would come. She was sure of it. But she didn't say this to Jack. She knew better now than to tell a penniless stranger that she had money.

Jack returned to his contemplation of the fire. "I'm not going anywhere" was all he said.

Frankie left the shantytown and walked to a prosperous section of the city. She didn't know how to go about finding a doctor, and was afraid to approach people on the street after her experiences earlier that day. She walked until she saw, outside a well-tended house, a shingle that read: CHARLES TAFT, M.D.—HOURS BY APPOINTMENT.

She climbed the steps and rang the buzzer. After a moment, a woman in a white nurse's uniform came to the door. As soon as she saw Frankie, her expression grew stern and disapproving. Before Frankie had a chance to speak, the woman said, "We don't give handouts here."

The door was closing in Frankie's face. Quickly she said, "Please, ma'am, I don't want a handout. I'm looking for a doctor."

The woman peered through the narrow crack of the doorway and said, "Dr. Taft is busy. He can't see every Tom, Dick, and Harry who comes in off the street."

"But I can pay!" Frankie cried frantically as the door shut the rest of the way. She turned to leave, then spun around and yelled, "And his name is *James*!"

She continued to walk the streets, growing more and more discouraged as she was turned away at one door after another. The short December day was growing dark when she happened upon a large brick hospital. With a cry of relief, she ran through the front door and up to the reception desk.

Frankie explained what she wanted, making sure to say that she had money and would pay. The woman behind the desk replied, "Bring your friend in and a doctor will see him."

"But I can't," said Frankie. "He's too sick."

"I'm very sorry," the woman said. She did look sorry. "But there's nothing I can do unless you bring him here. If he comes here, we'll do everything we can for him."

Frankie walked out the front door of the hospital. On the street, she burst into sobs of fury and frustration. She walked through the darkening streets, ignoring the stares of the people she passed.

After several blocks, she forced herself to grow calm and think. She had to get Stewpot to the hospital. There must be a way. A taxi!

On a busy downtown street, Frankie waved at five different cabs, but the drivers appeared not to see her. Finally, she took a couple of bills out of her pocket and waved them at the next taxi. The driver pulled over. When she asked to go to Hooverville, he asked to see her money again. Wearily, she handed him a dollar.

When he pulled up at the outskirts of Hooverville, she said, "Keep the change. And if you'll wait here, I'll be right back. Then I want to go to the hospital."

She hurried to Jack's shelter and found him where she had left him, staring into the dwindling fire. He looked up at Frankie's tear-streaked face and didn't say a word. She went past him into the room to check on Stewpot.

"Stew?" she said softly. Stewpot lay still, his breathing loud and ragged in the small, close space. "Stew? Wake up, we're going to the hospital."

Stewpot didn't answer or even open his eyes. Frightened, Frankie called, "Jack, there's a taxi waiting. I'm taking Stewpot to the hospital. Will you help me carry him?"

Jack pushed past the rug into the room. "Frank," he said hesitantly. Just then, Stewpot made a gurgling sound and began to cough and choke, his body heaving, as if someone were shaking him by the shoulders. His eyes remained shut. The spasm passed, and a reddish brown froth appeared at his mouth. Sobbing, Frankie wiped the spittle away with her coat sleeve.

"Help me!" she screamed, frantic now. Placing her hands beneath Stewpot's shoulders, she looked up at Jack. "Grab his feet!"

"You really got a cab?" asked Jack, eyeing her warily.

"Yes! *Just help me!*"

Together they carried Stewpot's limp body through the darkness, past the flickering shadows made by fires and oil lamps, to the edge of the shantytown. It seemed to take forever, and Stewpot's body was a dull, dead weight. Frankie was relieved to see the cab, still waiting in the same spot.

She leaned close to Stewpot and whispered happily, "You'll be at the hospital in no time, Stew." But her relief turned quickly to dismay when she looked into his eyes. They were dim and unseeing; his expression was oddly blank. Alarmed, she pressed her ear to his chest. Instead of harsh, ragged breathing, there was only silence.

"*Stewpot! No!*"

Twenty-five

The night was a long, dark tunnel into which Frankie fell. She sat on the floor of Jack's shack with Stewpot's head in her lap. She knew he was dead, and yet for a time she continued to believe that any minute he would open his eyes, flash his grin, and say, "This place is a dump. Let's blow outta here, Blue." Finally, as the night wore on, she gave up hope and simply sat, staring into the darkness, stunned with sorrow.

Jack woke up and looked at her. "I'm sorry, Frank," he said. "That's the way it is with pneumonia. You did everything you could."

His words didn't comfort Frankie. Jack didn't know that

she could have taken Stewpot to her aunt's house days ago, when he might have had a chance to recover. If only she had tried harder to talk him into it! If only she hadn't given in so easily.

"Guess we better get busy," said Jack.

Frankie's brain was dull and sluggish, and Jack's words had no meaning. She watched him as he got out of bed, pushed aside the rug in the doorway, and disappeared. Frankie continued to sit with Stewpot's head in her lap.

When Jack returned, a shovel with a broken handle in his hand, she looked at him blankly and didn't move. Jack put the shovel down, bent, and lifted Stewpot, still wrapped in his blanket, out of her arms. "Bring the shovel, Frank," he said, in a voice that was gruff, but not unkind.

Feeling as if she were in a dream, Frankie followed Jack to the far edge of the vacant lot, near a row of spindly poplar trees. There were three graves, one marked by a handmade wooden cross, one by a crudely lettered sign, and one, a ragged doll.

"Illegal, probably," said Jack with a shrug. "But what else are we going to do?"

Frankie stood by in a daze while Jack dug. When the hole was deep enough, Jack took Stewpot's blanket and spread it across the bottom, then lowered the body into the hole and started to wrap the blanket over Stewpot's face.

"Wait," said Frankie. Her voice was a faint croak.

Jack looked at her. "Want to say something?" he asked.

193

Frankie stared at him.

"You know, like a prayer?"

A prayer? thought Frankie. To whom? To God, who had allowed Stewpot to die? To President Hoover, who didn't seem to care that people were dying in desperate places named after him?

She was afraid that if she spoke, she would scream and scream and never stop. She was afraid of the terrible sadness that was filling her chest and her throat, and she pushed it down, as far down inside her as she could.

In its place, an anger rose. She could feel it building and was grateful. It was better to be angry. It made her feel strong.

Words came from her mouth in short, hard bursts. "It's wrong," she gasped. "All of—this." Her arms flew out, taking in the grave, the whole of Hooverville, the city of Seattle, and beyond. "He didn't have to die—he *shouldn't have died!*"

Tears fell steadily from her eyes as she thought about Stewpot. He had shown her his spirit, his courage, and his humor. She wondered if she would be able to find those qualities in herself in the days ahead. She had no idea how she would do it, but she promised Stewpot right then and there that she would try.

Bending down, she took the knife from Stewpot's pocket and put it into his hand. "A 'bo needs a knife," he had told her with his wide grin. Wherever Stewpot was now, or wherever he was going, she wanted him to have it.

Not caring what Jack might think, Frankie leaned over and kissed Stewpot's cold cheek, then gently covered him with his blanket. She rose and put her hands into her coat pockets, where her fingers closed around her harmonica. She remembered the first night she had met Stewpot, when he'd said, "That's a mighty sweet song, Frankie Blue."

Raising the harmonica to her lips, she played "Amazing Grace," Stewpot's favorite, as sweetly and gently as she could.

Then she and Jack pushed the dirt back into the hole. When they had finished, Jack leaned on the shovel and said flatly, "Let me tell you something, Frank. You say what's happening is wrong. Well, get used to it. The swells run the world. They're the ones who could make it better." He laughed abruptly. "If they wanted to."

Frankie didn't answer, and Jack went on. "People like us, we can't change anything. Look around." His mouth curved into a bitter smile. "Most of us can't even change our clothes."

Jack turned to leave. "You can stay if you want," he said. "But I can't feed you."

Frankie nodded, her mind elsewhere. "Thank you," she said absently. Jack may have heard her or not; he was already walking away.

Frankie didn't know how long she remained there. When she finally moved, she was stiff with cold and dizzy with hunger, but her steps were sure and unwavering. At Jack's shelter, she looked through Stewpot's bundle for anything that might tell her how to get in touch with his family. Surely Mrs. Haskell would want to know where her son was buried. But there was nothing. Frankie took the little box and the two wooden toys Stewpot had carved, and put them in her bag.

She bid Jack goodbye, then headed toward the railroad station. As she walked, she thought about what Jack had said and decided he was wrong. She refused to get used to a world where poor people died in places like Hooverville. It seemed to her that Jack had given up, just as Murph and her father had. They had let hopelessness move right into their hearts and take over. But Stewpot hadn't let that happen, and she wasn't about to, either.

Frankie moved through the train station as inconspicuously as possible, looking for the ladies' room. There she washed her hands and face and changed from her dirty clothing back into the blouse, stockings, and pinafore from her bag. Examining her reflection in the mirror, she saw a strange mixture of Frankie Blue and Frances Barrow. She didn't really care what she looked like; she merely wished to blend in with the other passengers, who were clean and well dressed for their journeys.

It felt odd to walk into the train station and right up to

the ticket window. "How much is it for a one-way ticket to Chicago?" she asked.

The clerk checked his tables. "It's forty dollars for coach. You'd have to sit the whole way, of course. Another eight twenty-five and you get a tourist berth in the sleeping car."

Frankie had forty-three dollars and sixty-five cents left. Luckily, it was enough for a seat. After sleeping in boxcars, sitting the whole way to Chicago on a soft, upholstered seat in a heated car sounded like the height of luxury. There was food on the train, and she'd have money left over to buy some. "One-way coach to Chicago will be fine," she said.

The clerk handed her the ticket, saying, "Train leaves at three-fifteen. Track four."

Frankie bought a ham sandwich and some hot chocolate and sat in the waiting area. It felt peculiar to mingle with the other passengers inside the warm station and to board the train along with them. Taking a seat by herself, she turned her face to the window and cried for Stewpot.

The warmth of the car and the softness of the seat enveloped her and, in her exhaustion, she finally slept.

Twenty-six

$\mathcal{F}$our days later, the train arrived at Union Station in Chicago. Frankie stood for a while on the street outside the station, just looking around. Stewpot had been to Chicago lots of times. Maybe he had once stood in the very same place, on the very same sidewalk. She liked to think that he had.

She liked knowing, too, that Big Chi was a crossroads for hoboes from every part of the country. Junius had promised her that if he went tramping, he'd show up at her Aunt Bushnell's door. She felt her face lift in a smile at the thought.

After asking a passerby directions to her aunt's street, she decided to walk there, even though it was several miles north of the station. She was used to walking. It would give her a chance to get a feel for this new city, and to think about what she would say when she was actually face-to-face with Aunt Bushnell.

Frankie wasn't afraid, but she knew that her aunt had good reason to be angry with her. Frankie had, after all, caused her aunt weeks of worry, and for that she would try to make amends. The odd thing was, she no longer felt like the same girl who had run away so thoughtlessly, without any idea of where she was headed or what she was leaving behind. Now that she had met Vera, Dot, Plain Jane, Blink, Peg-Leg Al, and all the others, she knew how foolish she had been to envy their lives, and to think hers was so hard. Compared to the 'boes she had met, she was lucky. She had a place to go. In time, she would learn to call it home.

And yet she was not at all sorry about her days on the road. How could she regret having known Stewpot? How could she regret that Frances Elizabeth Barrow had discovered what it was like to be Frankie Blue?

She thought she'd be ready, but when she finally reached her aunt's street, her stomach began to flutter and her steps slowed. She lingered on the sidewalk, taking careful notice of every detail of the neighborhood.

The stately brick and stone houses had tall windows covered by curtains and shutters drawn against the December chill. A wreath decorated one door, a sprig of holly another.

With a start, Frankie realized that Christmas would be coming soon.

She stopped in front of her aunt's house and gazed up at the windows, trying to picture what it was like inside. Junius had said she'd be able to continue her music lessons in Chicago. She hoped Aunt Bushnell had a piano.

Hitching her bag firmly across her shoulders, she took a deep breath and stepped up to the gate to let herself in. A mark on the white paint of the gatepost caught her eye. As she stepped closer to examine it, her eyes widened in disbelief.

Scratched into the wooden post was a crude picture of a cat: two circles, with pointed ears and whiskers, stick legs, and a tail. Frankie checked the address again, and an incredulous laugh burst from her mouth. She stared with amazement at the sign left for his fellow travelers by an unknown hobo.

A weight she hadn't realized she was carrying seemed to fall from her shoulders. Unsure of how welcome she would be, she had tried to prepare herself for the worst. But she had never, ever imagined *this*.

She opened the gate and walked up the brick pathway to the door, her heart pounding with anticipation. After taking one more deep breath, she reached for the heavy brass door knocker, and let it fall.